HAND ME DOWN LOVE

A SECOND CHANCE SURPRISE PREGNANCY ROMANCE

CHLOE BISHOP

A SECOND CHANCE THAT NEVER SHOULD HAVE HAPPENED

As soon as Matthew King walked back into my life, looking devastatingly handsome and completely irresistible, I should have shown him the door.

Instead, I let him deceive me.

The cost of that deception? Two little pink lines and that same man insisting that he can be the father our child needs.

I need to protect my heart. But in a small town like Rainbow Valley, there's no escaping a charming rogue like Matthew King.

So what can I possibly do when he's playing the dutiful father-to-be and insisting that our love was real all along?

Hand Me Down Love is a second chance, small town, surprise pregnancy romance with plenty of passionate baby-making, sweet nothings, and an HEA.

CHAPTER 1

KATE

A shrill scream penetrated the walls of the small antique shop. My eyes found Everly, my assistant. She was looking at me wide-eyed, waiting for the inevitable sound that typically followed such a sound.

It wasn't an unusual occurrence in the shop, but it usually heralded one thing.

CRASH!

Jumping to our feet, Everly and I rushed toward the front of the shop. The wail of a child punctuated the crash. It was the type of sound that always made my hair stand on end.

As we neared the wailing child, I saw that a collection of hardback books I'd spent an hour stacking attractively lay in shambles on the floor. As much as I wanted to sit and mourn the loss of another hour, I knew I had to attend to the customers at the center of the fray. Turning, I saw a mother holding a screaming toddler while the exasperated father stood behind her. He cringed as he looked from the mess on the floor then back at me.

"Is everyone alright?" I asked. I was meticulous about my displays and the layout of the store. Every step I took, I considered how a customer might interact with a product or fixture. One thing I always asked myself was, "is the shop safe?" I thought of sharp edges, narrow passageways, and items too high to retrieve. Then, I tried to ensure that there was no way a customer could get hurt.

Not always an easy feat in an antique shop.

As I waited for either the mother or father to answer my question, I tried to figure out how the toddler toppled the display of books. The books were well out of the reach of a toddler, but there was still that chance that one sat too close to the table's edge.

"We're fine," the mother finally answered. I recognized her expression. It was the one I wore when I dealt with my sister for longer than an hour. Or God forbid, my mother.

"I was holding him," she continued as the toddler wailed, squirming and trying to remove himself from her hold. "I don't know how he managed it, but somehow he did. I'm so sorry."

Behind them, the father blew out a breath. Something told me he'd been holding it as he waited to see what his wife would say.

"Don't worry about it," I said, meaning it. The books would wait until later. The important thing was that no one was hurt. "Why don't you sit over in the furniture section and I'll fix you some tea. I have some snacks in the back that might help him feel a little calmer."

I looked toward the squirming toddler as I said it, but I could have as easily meant the father, who looked done with the whole charade.

"Oh, we couldn't impose," she said, her cheeks pink. Obviously, she'd expected a dragon when I'd rushed toward the chaos. "We should help you clean up."

"Nonsense," I said. Truth was, I would much rather put things to rights myself than depend on a customer to do so. "Don't worry about the display. I'd feel much better about you guys taking a breather."

I settled the couple with tea and snacks inside a small alcove where customers could appreciate the atmosphere of the shop. With the couple settled, I returned to the pile of books.

I tilted my head, wondering if there was some way to make the display even more user-friendly.

"Whatever you're thinking, there's no way that you could have made that display anymore toddler-proof than it already was," Everly mumbled as she came to stand behind me. I'd hired Everly as my assistant as soon as I'd bought the antique shop. When I'd purchased the shop, it had been an aging business with little hope of prosperity. My mother warned me against my foolishness, in her words, of buying the shop. After all, it was destined to fail.

But somehow, the shop became my dream. And since my greatest dream had fallen apart only a few years before I'd bought the shop, I wasn't about to let another one slip through my fingers. Not when this one's success depended only on me.

The former owner hadn't expected the shop to sell. A developer in town was keen on buying the shop and those next to it. Once he purchased it, he planned to raze all the shops and build condos. It was only the original shopkeeper's stubbornness that persuaded him to sell to me instead of the developer, at a lesser cost. The original owner knew, rightly so, that if the antique shop went to the developer, the rest of the shops would soon follow suit.

Old Things New had never been a truly lucrative business. While I'd kept the shop in the black, I still barely made ends meet. It was pure stubbornness that kept the shop open and Everly paid a salary that she was worth.

Everly and I stacked the books as the front door dinged with the arrival of a new customer. An older couple stepped in and I greeted them warmly. They were tourists to Rainbow Valley. They came for the sensational rainbow shows that occurred near the lake. And usually, while they were in town, they partook of the town's quaint shopping district. Most of my business - at least that which wasn't online - was courtesy of the tourists who traveled through.

I looked back over my shoulder toward the couple with the toddler. They were unaware of my attention. I fought back that same jealous spark that burbled in the pit of my stomach anytime I saw a young family. It was a petty jealousy. One that sparked anger toward the man who'd destroyed my chance at having my own family.

I could have moved on. Could have found someone else and started a family. But he'd always overshadowed everyone I'd considered in his wake.

"Excuse me."

Turning in the voice's direction, I saw the woman who'd stepped into the shop earlier. She stood before the counter and pointed to a set of L. Frank Baum books displayed behind the counter. I nearly groaned.

"How much for the L. Frank Baum books?" she asked.

"Unfortunately, someone else has already claimed them. They've just haven't come in and pick them up. I'm so sorry."

The woman's shoulders slumped, filling me with a fresh bout of guilt. Just as it always did when I'd to tell someone the books were not for sale. I'd once told customers who inquired that they were for display only. This prompted a few customers to try and wheel and deal me out of the books. After a while, I began using the same excuse.

They belonged to another customer. Already paid for.

I never explained that the other customer was me.

After the couple left, finding a few other items that they'd been unable to live without, Everly leaned against the counter and fixed me with that look. Everly was much too good at reading people. It had made her a success with the store's social media presence. Somehow, she understood what people wanted to see online. Her work on the store's social platforms made the store fairly successful online. I wouldn't be buying a yacht soon, but it brought in extra revenue. Enough extra revenue that I was at least able to justify paying Everly a decent salary.

"Why don't you just take the books home?" Everly asked. "At least then you wouldn't have that guilty look on your face when you have to tell yet another customer that you can't sell the books."

I shrugged. "I like the way they look. They're a conversation piece. Besides, it gives the impression that customers are vying for our merchandise when I tell them I have customers paying for stuff in advance."

Lies, lies, lies. And unfortunately, Everly knew it.

Luckily, she didn't realize the real reason, at least. That I'd bought them before there was ever a shop. When I was young and in love.

When dreams of little babies and reading those books to them had danced in my head.

Then, that love had gone sour.

I didn't take the books home because I knew what I'd do once I got them there. I'd pick them up each night before I went to bed and dream of a time I still had a promise of that dream. And I couldn't invite that possibility back into my life.

THE TINY LITTLE bungalow I'd bought once I'd socked away enough money for a down payment was nothing like the dream house I'd once envisioned. Two bedrooms, a small kitchen, and a small living area were definitely not luxury living. But I loved it because it was mine.

I'd added cozy little touches that made it look like something between an English cottage and a tiny vacation getaway. If I squinted, I could imagine that each day I was stepping into my own little vacation home.

The neighbors were close, but not too close, giving me enough yard to plant an herb garden. Of course, more times than not, that herb garden had suffered from lack of attention. I'd also placed a little seating area out back that made for comfortable seating when the weather was warmer. Given that it was early June, I could at least spend some time outside enjoying the weather in my little cone of privacy.

Taking a seat at the little patio table, I pushed my feet up on the opposite chair and leaned my head back, watching the fireflies buzz through the backyard.

Everly had a point. If I took the books home, I wouldn't be so melancholy after someone bothered to inquire about them. I'd hide them in a box - as if I had the space for anything else in my tiny house - and pretend they didn't exist.

Or, I could get on with my life and sell them to the next person who inquired about them.

That felt like giving up on that dream. Matthew might be gone, but I couldn't let go of that dream we'd shared altogether. Babies and that big house out on Cadence Road. If everything had gone the way I'd planned, I wouldn't be in my tiny garden paradise with the fireflies zooming overhead. I'd be home with him. Maybe we would have a few kids by now. The years would have given us time to make a few, that was for sure. Perhaps we'd only had boys or girls and would be trying to break the pattern.

Matthew and I had been good at the trying part. We'd also been smart about it, which was why at thirty, I was still without that mythical baby.

My phone trilled, pulling me from my thoughts of what-ifs. For a moment, I was glad to have something to distract me until I saw the number on the screen.

"Hi, Mom," I chirped as I brought the phone to my ear. Not that I disliked my mother. We just had one of those strange relationships. The one where no matter what I said, my mother seemed to do her best not to understand any of it.

"You're not still at the old things shop, are you?"

I sighed. Ever since I'd bought the shop, my mother refused to call it anything other than "the old things shop." While the title was technically true, I knew it was my mother's way of voicing her displeasure with the way my life had gone.

"I'm home. Just sitting outside enjoying the evening."

Or I had been.

"Fantastic, Kate. Because I have fabulous news!" The fevered pitch of my mother's voice caused me to pull the phone away from my ear. I made sure the number was still my mother's, and that it hadn't magically changed to some other contact entirely. My mother rarely showed excitement. My father once joked that even when she'd given birth to my sister and me, she'd mostly just let out a grunt and then a relieved sigh.

"Cassie is getting married!" The words were all but screamed into my ear.

Cassie was my little sister. Ever since her arrival into the Cavanaugh clan, Cassie had been the darling of my parents' eye. I'd merely been the tester model they'd used to ensure they got everything right for Cassie.

I wasn't bitter. Not most of the time. Though I wondered if my mother would have been nearly as excited about my own wedding.

I didn't have time to respond to my mother's exclamation before I heard my sister's voice chirp in.

"And, of course, you'll be my maid of honor," Cassie interjected.

My mother had an annoying habit of calling me with Cassie on the line and failing to mention Cassie's presence. While I couldn't imagine any scenario in which I would feel comfortable chatting about Cassie with my mother, I was still always careful with my words while I was on the phone with Mom.

"Of course I will," I automatically supplied. It had always been a given that Cassie would have a big wedding. It had also always been a given that I would be her maid of honor. Not so much because the two of us were close. Unfortunately, we weren't. It was more because our mother would demand it. Cassie also knew that I would roll over and do whatever was needed to ensure there was as little conflict as possible.

I listened, waiting for the moments between Cassie and my mother's verbal diarrhea. Occasionally, I'd add a grunt of affirmation or a 'hmm' of understanding. At one point in my life, I'd dreamt of a huge wedding with all the bells and whistles, just like Cassie was planning. When the guy I'd been planning on sharing that wedding with had exited my life, I ditched all those plans. Now, I wasn't even sure I'd want that big wedding. Perhaps it was hindsight, but now I imagined something smaller. More intimate. Something where love was the main ingredient instead of the length of my train.

When the call finally ended, I let out a sigh of relief. Throughout the night, my phone buzzed with texts. Cassie was already pummeling my texts with links to various dresses, asking for my opinion. As if she would actually take my opinion into account.

Still, as I looked through the dresses, I tried to view them with as critical an eye as possible. I was no fashion maven. I knew how to look good, but had no clue what wedding fashion was these days. It had been at least ten years since I'd perused a bridal website or looked through a wedding magazine.

Cassie had a style she seemed to prefer. Cassie was sleek and tall. Her figure would hold up to just about any dress, but she could pull off the tight, sleek designs that some other brides couldn't. Cassie knew this, too. All the gowns she was sending through were beautiful.

They were not, however, the type of gown I would gravitate toward. Giving in to temptation, I clicked through the other dresses on the site that Cassie had shared. I was curious to see what styles they offered.

Most of the dresses were either too fashion-forward or too extravagant. One dress, however, caught my eye. It was a simple, vintage-style gown, because of course it was. It had a sweetheart neckline that would have accentuated my cleavage and a tapered waist that would have complimented my waistline.

I shook my head. As if I was going to be in the market for a wedding gown anytime soon.

I could, of course, show the dress to my sister. No doubt, she would find it not to her liking and reject it. Despite that, there was something about it that made me not want to send it to Cassie. It was as if it belonged to me, even though I knew I'd never wear the thing.

In truth, it reminded me a lot of the gown I'd once picked out when I thought I would walk down the aisle toward a waiting Matthew King. I closed my eyes. I could still envision him standing there, smiling at me. It was a vision I'd entertained too many times. Before we'd broken up, I'd thought of that scenario just about every night as I laid my head on my pillow. And, admittedly, the vision popped into my head uninvited more than a few times since we'd broken up.

I'd tried to stop imagining that years ago. But now, looking at the site, those old dreams came rushing back to the forefront. I was going to have to get my head in the game, push away all those old thoughts and make this solely about my sister. It would be the only way I could make it through the next eight months of planning.

What I would need to remind myself of was the fact that Matthew wasn't sitting around thinking of me. Even though Rainbow Valley wasn't a big town, I rarely saw him. I knew this was in part because of my avoiding the places that I knew he liked to frequent. I had a horrible memory of going to dinner one night alone and seeing him there with a date. He hadn't seen me, so I'd rushed out before there was a chance of an awkward confrontation.

No. I wouldn't let these thoughts destroy me over the next year. There weren't enough antacids in town to get through putting myself through that.

And yet, I still bookmarked that dress. I wasn't sure why I did. I felt stupid for doing it. But for some reason, I just couldn't let it go. Maybe one of these days, I could let go of Matthew King and find love with someone else.

CHAPTER 2

MATTHEW

Ask just about anyone in town and they'll tell you that Matthew King knows how to read people. It was a trait that had served me well and made me the most successful real estate broker in Rainbow Valley. I knew when to charm. Knew when to bully and when to walk away. Eat your heart out, Kenny Rogers.

In the seven years I'd spent building my business, I'd done my best to always walk away from Ted Palmer. Ted was a ruthless developer. A man who bought land and buildings just to rip them apart and see what he could extract from them. It didn't matter if his actions put the entire town at risk. It was the thrill of the conquest that attracted him.

As a businessman, I suffered him as politely as possible. Ted knew I had no designs on a friendship or partnership with him. It was for this reason that he and I spent most of our time avoiding each other.

Which was how I knew that Ted's presence in my office was nothing but trouble.

"Don't pretend like you're not surprised to see me in your office, Matthew," Ted said as he took a seat across from my desk. I'd done well for myself, but I had no desire to look like it. My office was a little bungalow in the downtown area. It was small, unassuming, and didn't fill my clients with trepidations when they stepped inside.

Ted, in contrast, had built a three-story brick monstrosity on the outskirts of town. It was a building that looked both modern and outdated. It was impersonal, much like Ted.

"What brings you here today, Ted?" I asked, fixing the older man with an inscrutable stare. I could have asked for tea or coffee to be brought to him. I didn't. It was Ted, and I wanted nothing more than to be finished with the ensuing conversation.

"I want to revisit the possibility of purchasing the Brinkley land."

I didn't blink. I didn't swallow. I did nothing that would give my thoughts away. Instead, I watched the man before me, cataloging every twitch, every breath.

"None of the business owners are interested in selling," I managed.

Project calm, Matthew. Poise. I wouldn't let him know how loudly the alarm bells in my head were clanging . "Hell, you know the business owners don't want to sell. There's no way to force them out. They've been steady on this for years."

"They've been steady on this for years because there's one among them who spurs them on toward staying in place," Ted said, his eyes unwavering from my stare. Rainbow Valley was a small town. I knew why Ted had come to my office for this scheme. There were pros and cons to small town living. One of the cons was that everyone knew your history just about as well as you did.

"In fact," Ted continued, "had she not purchased that failing shop, I suspect I'd already have the complex on that land that I want. I could be convincing tourists to move here instead of them buying a few silly trinkets and then watching as they moved on with their lives."

Ted was still talking, but I was sticking on that one word. She.

There wasn't a day that went by that I didn't try to avoid thinking about Kate Cavanaugh. It had been ten years since we'd parted ways and every day of those ten years had been an exercise in preventing her from taking over my mind completely.

And now Ted Palmer was here, bringing her up without even saying her name.

"Be that as it may, Ted, you've just admitted that there's little chance that they will sell. So why are you here?"

Ted smirked. It was a slimy smirk. Ted had a way of smiling that could either make you feel like he was your best friend or your worst enemy. Right now, he was using the latter smile as he stared at me.

"I thought if anyone could talk this particular business owner into selling, it would be you. And once she succumbs and sells, the others would follow suit."

It was damned hard not to swallow around the invisible rock that had formed in my throat. Still, despite the discomfort with the situation, I wasn't sure why Ted would think that I could persuade Kate to sell Old Things New. Furthermore, I didn't know why Ted thought I would help him. Did he think I harbored some ill will toward Kate?

Did Kate believe that, too?

I pushed the thought aside that there was an excellent possibility that she just might.

"I doubt very much that I'm the person who could help you with that," I said, leaning back in my chair and trying appear as nonchalant as possible. "Besides, and not to be rude, but why would I even want to help you?"

"Because I may have something you want." The words left Ted's lips like a threat. And I knew, in a way that didn't involve kidnappings or murders, Ted must mean it as such. Ted wouldn't dare make such a statement if he didn't think he could follow through on it.

"I can't imagine there's anything you have that I want, but please inform me of what this thing is so we can move past these soap opera dramatics, Ted."

Ted's smile broadened. He knew he was getting under my skin and as much as I wanted to pretend that he wasn't, my hands were clammy and my throat was dry. I knew the bastard knew how much I wanted to throttle him.

"I have the Richardson Estate."

It was an innocuous statement. No different from "I had coffee for breakfast." But Ted knew how volatile the statement was. He likely also knew I wanted to kill him.

As it was, I was fighting the urge to jump up from my seat and toss him out of the office. I knew my face must have been growing red. I was clenching my fists, wanting to send one of them right through Ted's smiling face.

"I know how badly you wanted that place," Ted continued, his smile never wavering. I was beginning to wonder how I would explain to a judge why Ted's face needed rearranging. "So, I figured I could make you a deal. You help me get the Brinkley land where that development sits and I'll sell the Richardson place to you."

Then Ted shrugged. Such a benign motion, but it was edged with malice. "If not, I'll have to raze the house on the estate. It's old. Weathered. Very few people want it. I'll have to do something with the land, I suppose. Something to serve as a salve to my disappointment at not getting exactly what I want."

He sighed.

Asshole.

"I don't understand," I said, finally. My voice was much too quiet. It mirrored nothing of what I was feeling on the inside. "I was under the impression that the current owner was keen on keeping the estate."

Granted, it had been awhile since I had actually checked. But still, it made no sense. None of it. Currently, the old farmhouse was vacant. Probably rotting. It was a damned shame.

"You should know by now that I get what I want, Matthew." Not once did Ted show any sign of discomfort. There was no flare of his nostrils. No nervous twitching. He was stoic. Complete bastard through and through.

"Look, Matthew. I'm not trying to come across as a villain."

Somehow, I managed not to snort.

"You can look at it this way: I've helped you get something you've always wanted. Now, you only have to help me in return."

"And what would you have me do?" I hated myself for even asking the question. I'd somehow kept my tells to a minimum. Showed no signs of disappointment. I sat, staring across at the man as if I were completely unbothered by this chain of events. Perhaps in a few years, I might even be a complete bastard like Ted.

I hoped not.

"Talk to her. Convince her it's a losing game." Ted said the words as if it was a foregone conclusion that I could convince Kate of anything, let alone give up the one dream she had left. "Tell her there are better things out there. Like a three-story Victorian where she can build the life she wants. You can sell it to her for a steal. She can buy it with the money that she makes from selling the shop."

That house hadn't been just Kate's dream. It had been mine as well.

I knew damn well that Ted knew that. I had to give him credit. He had done his homework.

"I'll speak to her," I said, finally. It felt as if I had just agreed to sign my death warrant. In some ways, perhaps I had.

"I make no promises, though."

THURSDAY NIGHTS WERE family dinner nights with the King family.

Over the years, I'd missed a few dinners. Usually, however, you didn't miss a dinner unless your head was falling off, or they had shipped you off to war.

My father died when I was 15. The loss had been devastating. He'd left behind my mother and three children who had continued to feel the loss of him every day. Peter King had been a larger-than-life man who remembered everyone's name. He knew if the postman's daughter was sick with the flu and never forgot to ask about her when he happened upon the man at the mailbox. He sent flowers to the funerals of people he'd had only cursory contact with throughout his life. He had instilled in his children the sense that people deserved respect, no matter who they were. His funeral had been a large affair and, during the visitation, a line had wrapped around the building as people waited to pay their respects.

Peter King's life had been an example for his children to follow.

It was why I felt I was always coming up short. I wasn't a Ted Palmer, wheeling and dealing and using people's dreams and weaknesses against them. While I'd been more than successful, I'd achieved that success by listening to people and trying to help them realize their dreams. Whether that dream was a three-bedroom family home or a warehouse from which to start their own business.

I had attempted to follow in my father's footsteps, which had led to my success. There was a reason I didn't travel in the same circles as Ted Palmer.

There were even more reasons I never did business with him.

"You look constipated," Sophie said as I walked through the front door of my childhood home.

"Maybe I am," I retorted. Sophie was only 23, the youngest of my siblings. She had made a name for herself online as a popular cosplayer. I paid as little attention as possible to her social media. It was enough that her outfits were the type of thing you never wanted to see your sister wearing. The comments beneath those photos were enough to drive a big brother to madness.

I'd gotten as far as finding out the locations of some commenters before I pulled myself back from doing something stupid.

The vagaries of how she made money dressing up as fictional characters perplexed me, but there was no doubt she had been a success at it.

As I ventured further into the two-story home where I'd grown up, I could hear the others near the back of the house where the dining room was. I heard my older brother's deep, throaty laugh and my younger sister's exclamation in response. The gang was all here.

Part of me wanted to be alone with my thoughts. But as I stepped into the familiar sights and sounds of the King family home, I was glad to be with family. For a little while, it would keep my mind away from the conniving machinations of Ted Palmer.

It would keep my mind off Kate and what had once been our dream.

Still, even though I wanted to drown myself in the happiness of my family being around me, I couldn't keep my mind off the things that had happened earlier. Of the memories it had brought to mind.

"Alright, tell me why you look so constipated," Sophie said as we sat on the back patio, sipping iced tea and watching the fireflies buzz across the lawn. Summer was just beginning. It was the kind of night that made me want a drink with a little more punch, especially considering the thoughts running through my mind. Right now, iced tea would have to do.

My mother, who was sitting nearby, was pretending not to listen to Sophie grilling me. She was also doing a piss-poor job of appearing not to eavesdrop.

I had no intention of telling them everything. Telling them how I was tearing myself apart inside when I thought of what Ted Palmer had laid at my feet earlier. Sophie had been young when I'd been with Kate, but she'd still taken to her as most did to Kate. Sophie, like the rest of us, had mourned Kate's absence from their lives. In the past, Kate had been a fixture at King family dinners. It was a thought that tickled at the back of my brain every Thursday night as I sat around laughing with my family. It always felt like something was missing. I didn't doubt that I felt it more keenly than anyone. Though, some-times a phantom lull appeared in the conversation. It was as if we were all waiting for Kate to offer her thoughts on whatever it was we were talking about.

"Ted Palmer has purchased the Richardson Estate," I finally said, my voice flat.

All pretense of my mother not listening to my conversation with Sophie flew out the window as she let out a gasp.

I knew I didn't have to say anything else to them. They knew what the place meant to me. What it had represented. Even Sophie, who had been a mere child when Kate and I had broken up, knew the importance of the Richardson Estate. Knew what I hoped it would become one day.

"That sleaze," Sophie said. "He always likes all my photos."

That admission had me raising an eyebrow. "I thought you wanted people to like your photos," Adam said, stepping out onto the porch to join the conversation as it got juicy.

"He likes all of them," Sophie added, as if that should explain everything. Sophie was a beautiful girl, but never seemed to capitalize on it beyond what she did with her cosplay business. She was the type of girl who turned heads whether she was in jeans and a t-shirt or an evening gown. Not that she wore evening gowns all that often. It had been disconcerting to watch her go from a little girl with food stains on her face to this vixen, who caused men to stammer in her presence.

"I'm sure most guys like all your photos," Adam said.

"Yeah, but then, when he's around me, he acts like a complete asshole. Like, don't look at my photos, dude, if you're going to treat me like shit when you see me."

"Language," Mom admonished, but there was a smile on her face.

"Sorry. I'll not say photos again mother. Clearly, I meant pictures." This led to an argument on the differences between "photos" and "pictures." The argument then morphed into one on the difference between "shit" and "poop." It was nearly enough to forget what we had been talking about only moments before.

However, occasionally, my mother would give me that look. The one that told me she knew why I was so upset. Even if she believed I didn't realize it myself.

No matter how many years had passed since that fateful night, I would never move on. I would never be over Kate.

CHAPTER 3

KATE

Fridays were one of the busiest days of the week for Old Things New. With Rainbow Valley being an off-the-beaten-path tourist destination, people found their way to our town on their way to other destinations. While we weren't usually on the roster of their plans, they usually couldn't resist stopping in. The little shops were quaint looking. Although we were landlocked, the shops had the look of a Cape Cod village. All that was missing was the smell of saltwater in the air.

Most people stopped in to browse. Still, I made sure they left with the information for our online storefront and all our social media details. Some people actually bought something in the shop. Usually nothing more than a few nostalgic trinkets, but occasionally, someone bought a bigger ticket item.

"I saw Cassie is getting married," Everly said as we stood behind the counter during a lull. She used the time to check the store's Facebook and Instagram accounts, replying to messages or comments where necessary.

Of course Everly would know that Cassie was getting married. Cassie had posted the obligatory photo of her hand wearing her new ring right after our conversation. There was also one with her new fiancé.

"She texted me all night long." It wasn't an exaggeration. Once 10 pm had hit, I'd silenced the phone so I could get some sleep. Otherwise, she would have been texting me until one in the morning. "Pictures of wedding gowns. Cakes. Honeymoon destinations. Potential wedding venues."

I sighed. Everly gave me a look. The look.

"I'm going to ask a question and you have to promise you won't get mad about it."

Rolling my eyes, I didn't let Everly ask the question.

"I'm not jealous of my sister," I said, anticipating her question. "At least, not in the way you're thinking. I'm jealous but in a more abstract way. I don't begrudge her for her happiness. And I wouldn't want to be engaged to Mark myself, but it's more that I've missed out on these things myself."

Everly said nothing to this, for which I was glad. While she was good at calling me on my bullshit, she also didn't overstep. She'd gotten the truth out of me - at least the truth as far as I understood it. And I could have found someone else. Hell, I could have been married by now.

But I hadn't wanted to. Ten years later and I still wasn't over Matthew King. Perhaps that's how it was. If you're lucky enough to experience that feeling of being someone's one true love and them being yours, you don't get a second chance.

Maybe it hadn't stopped him from looking for his second chance, but for me, everything had paled in comparison. When you come so close to getting everything you ever wanted, only to have it snatched away, it's hard to come back from that. And I guess I never had.

And admittedly, there was another facet to my almost-jealousy that stemmed from my sister's wedding. I knew that for a year, the only thing we would eat, sleep, and drink in the Cavanaugh family would be Cassie's wedding. My mother was ecstatic and though I hadn't talked to my father, I knew he would approve of Cassie marrying one of the Jensen boys.

The Jensen family was a well-known family in Rainbow Valley. Mark ran his own financial consulting business and had done well for himself. Everything about the match seemed perfect. My sister could be high-strung, but he seemed to genuinely care about her, which pleased me as well.

Still, it would have been nice for my parents - and my sister as well - to show a little enthusiasm about the successes in my life. While Old Things New would never bear grandchildren or allow my mother to play mother to the bride, it had been my pride and joy. I'd worked hard to make it the modest success that it was. But to them, it was the "throw away shop" and that would likely burn for the rest of my life.

Hearing my phone vibrate against the wooden counter of the cash wrap, I picked it up and saw that I had a litter of unread texts from my sister. Likely more gowns or venues. Sighing, I put the phone under the register and returned my attention to the shop before me.

And that's when I saw him. He was standing near the door, watching me. Dressed in a suit that was tailored to fit every plane of his body, he looked tall and sleek and too well dressed to be in the antique shop. He hadn't yet taken off his sunglasses and, as if realizing that I'd noticed that, he pulled them off and I swallowed a gasp as I looked at him.

Matthew had never been to the shop. I'd bought the shop four years after Matthew and I had become history. He had no more business in my shop than I had in his office. I'd imagined this moment for years. Imagined how I would feel when he finally stood inside the walls of a dream I'd exchanged for the dream that I had wanted to share with him.

The antique shop had always been part of the dream. He was going to be an architect while I ran the shop. I swallowed, thinking about his dream of being an architect. After all, it was that dream that had ended ours.

And now, he wasn't an architect at all. Funny how all that had worked out.

I wasn't sure how long we stood there staring at one another.

"It's even better than I imagined," he said, breaking the tense silence.

"I'm surprised that you bothered to imagine it." I hadn't meant to sound so bitter. I'd dreamt of the first things I would say to him when I saw him again. Nothing coming out of my mouth was close to what I imagined. I'd imagined that I would be clever and uncaring. That I could somehow make it seem like our parting hadn't affected me as deeply as it had.

And with one sentence, I'd let all that anger and bitterness rise to the top, telling him exactly how much our parting had affected me. Had I been the calm and collected person I wished to be, I would have walked to him and feigned that we were simply old friends who had never parted.

That was out of the question now.

Pulling away from the door, he edged closer to me. I held my breath, wishing that I could seem completely unaffected by his sudden presence in my world. I wasn't sure when Everly had disappeared, but I found it hard to imagine that she wasn't somewhere in the shop, watching whatever drama this was unfolding.

He stopped a good five feet away from me, but his eyes never left my face.

"Of course I imagined it." His voice was thick. It seemed out of place with the calm he was projecting. He looked every inch the formidable businessman. And yet, I could remember him reluctantly admitting that "While You Were Sleeping" was one of his favorite movies.

"I imagined many things back then."

I narrowed my eyes. What was Matthew doing in my shop after ten years of separation? We'd both hit our thirties. Perhaps it was some sort of early midlife crisis that had him visiting his old flame.

Whatever had brought him here, I was not game for it. I was never going to get hurt like that again.

"What can I help you with, Mr. King?" There. Pure business. Sure, his presence affected me, but that didn't mean that I had to give into it. If I made this as impersonal as possible, I could keep a handle on the situation.

Of course, after saying his name in such a way, I remembered all the times I had called him that and he had referred to me as the future Mrs. King. I wondered if he remembered the same thing.

Right now, I was determined to discover why he was here.

"I've passed by here many times. I wanted to come in and see the place." He looked around, taking in all the details of the shop. It felt like he was assessing my body instead of the shop I had cultivated for so many years. And damn it, I wanted him to be impressed with what he saw. "I decided that today was the day I would give in and see what you've done with the place. It's amazing, Kate. You should be proud."

Part of me hated him at that moment. How many times had I wanted to hear him say those words to me? How many times had I envisioned the first time he would walk into my shop and see it and be proud of it in a way that my parents refused to be?

Damn him for giving me a glimpse of something I knew I'd never be able to have.

He'd believed in me. Told me I could do anything. There had been an indestructible faith there from the beginning.

Except for the one time that faith had utterly left him. When he believed I had sabotaged his chance at getting into the school for design that he had been dreaming of for years.

I wanted him to stay with me. That was true. I'd discouraged him when he talked about going off to school and finally becoming the architect he had dreamt of becoming. But I'd thought about all the ways it would pull us apart. I'd imagined him finding someone more worldly and sophisticated than me. Someone more interesting than a small-town girl who wanted to own an antique shop. I imagined him meeting a woman who shared his dreams. Someone who wanted to be an architect, just like him.

Or maybe she would be a quirky art student, vibrant and irresistible. I'd spent many a night imagining the day he would meet this imaginary woman who would sweep him off his feet and make him forget all about me.

I was young and in love and terrified of losing him.

But I never said a word. Not a word. I'd fallen in love, but I never wanted a man who had to be pressured to stay. I knew he would eventually resent me for pressuring him to forsake his dreams. Likewise, I would resent him because I would never know if he had truly chosen me.

So I'd said nothing.

In the end, it had been his mother who couldn't let him go. It was she who had hindered his chance by hiding the letter of acceptance he had received. She'd come to me after the blowup - after Matthew had confronted me, convinced that it was me who had done the deed. She'd told me all of it. How she had feared what might happen if he went away. Losing her husband had stung, and she didn't want what remained of her family scattered to the ends of the earth. So she'd hid the letter and watched the email account since he'd never closed his computer at night. She'd laughed when she told me how she was afraid she wouldn't be there to catch the email.

What she hadn't expected was that he would see that the email had been deleted and knew he would never have done it himself. The only explanation was that I had done it one night when I'd been in his room.

Because I was always in his room.

She explained her plans to set him straight. To tell him she had been the one to sabotage his plans, not me. She was weepy that day. Terrified that, in her haste to try not to lose her son, she had done the one thing that would actually cause him to flee her.

And so I'd begged her not to tell him. While I refused to take the blame, I also didn't want to see this tear them apart. He had the relationship with his mother that I'd wanted to have with my own. It made me somewhat glad for the gulf that had kept my mother and me from being close enough to create this sort of drama. My mother would never go to such strange and devious machinations to keep me close to her.

And thank God for that.

Furthermore, I had wanted him to trust me. Believe in me. I'd begged and pleaded for him to believe that I hadn't betrayed his trust. And he didn't believe me. There was nothing his mother could do to fix that. I hoped he would come to his senses. Hoped he would get past his upset and anger and realize that I could never do such a thing.

Even if I had been terrified of losing him.

In the end, I had lost him, and I'd done nothing to cause it.

And now he dared to come into my shop looking like walking sex. I couldn't remember ever thinking that he had looked like walking sex back when we had been together. Something had drawn me to him. I'd always found him attractive, but he was a boy back then. He was still a little lanky, a bit unsure of himself.

Now? He had filled out. The planes of his face had grown more angular, more masculine. And he carried himself like a man who had spent the last ten years making a name for himself. He had a confidence that came with experience. And standing before him made me feel like a green schoolgirl with a bruised self-esteem.

Would I even recognize all those parts of him I had one time memorized? It pained me to know that there were women in Rainbow Valley who knew his body better now than I did.

Calm yourself, Kate.

"Well, now you've seen the shop," I said, drawing myself back to the present. "What else can I do for you?"

"Can't I just come in and say hello, Kate?" The way he said my name sent liquid fire surging through my body, heading straight to that part which had once known his touch so intimately.

He couldn't just come in and say hello. Not without my body revolting against me.

Narrowing my eyes at him, I wouldn't let my body win this war. "What are you up to?"

He hesitated. I nearly panicked as I considered that I might have pushed him too far. But didn't I want him to leave so I could move on?

As if I had ever moved on.

I saw something vulnerable in his eyes. It was quick. So fleeting I barely had time to catch it. But it was there. Just a tiny glimpse of the boy he once was. The one who had made plans with me to live in a big house and have lots of babies.

"I know it's been a long time," he said. I repressed a snort. "But I was wondering if we could grab lunch."

Not at all what I was expecting. And I still didn't trust it or understand it. He'd once refused to believe me and now I was returning the favor.

I wouldn't find out what he was about if I didn't go along with whatever this was.

It had nothing to do with the fact that I wanted to spend time with him. He had occupied my thoughts for ten years after he had left my life. Curiosity won out.

"Alright." The word stuck in my throat.

"What do you say to Something to Eat at 2?" he suggested.

It wasn't quite neutral ground. At least not for him. Something to Eat was the restaurant next door to the shop, keeping the "thing" theme going in the little shopping area. I doubt he realized that Mara Langdon was one of the town's biggest gossips and would listen to every word we said.

But she was loyal to me and if I needed her to save me from an unpleasant situation, I knew I could count on her.

"It's a…" I stopped myself. I had nearly said 'it's a date.' Hopefully, he hadn't caught that. The hint of a smirk told me he had. "That will work. I'll see you at 2."

I turned around, leaving him alone in the store.

CHAPTER 4

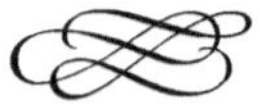

MATTHEW

As soon as I'd stepped into the shop and saw her, my breath left me. She was gorgeous. Even more gorgeous than she'd been when we'd been ten years younger and madly in love.

So, my feelings hadn't changed. How had I made it this long without being near her?

I'd tried to move on. There had been dates. There had been relationships.

But they had never been Kate. Every date, I was waiting for her to show up, which was fair to no one.

I'd stopped being angry at Kate years ago. Hell, I'd stopped being angry a week after the blowup. It had only been my pride that had kept me away. I'd been determined to teach her a lesson. I was convinced that if I waited her out, she'd come to me, confess all, and we could move on.

She had been terrified of losing me. Terrified that I'd go off to school and find someone who would make me forget all about her. The joke was on both of us. Ten years later and I still had found no one who could make me forget Kate. She haunted my dreams. Mocked any plans I tried to make.

As time went on, it wasn't the loss of my school acceptance that kept me away from her. It was the memory of how devastated she'd looked when I refused to believe her. I couldn't get past the fact that I was the one who had delivered that final blow.

I'd cheated myself out of watching her grow into this incredible woman. Her features had grown sharper. Her body had filled out from the more angular lines of youth into something more womanly and even sexier.

Unfortunately, years of hurt and disappointment had turned that wide-eyed, innocent gaze into something more world-weary.

I'd missed out on seeing her achieve her dream of having her own antique shop. She'd always loved "old things." While her parents had found her eccentricities exasperating, they'd only made me love her more.

That she'd gone and turned those hobbies into something profitable was a testament to how resilient she was. She didn't have to tell me that her parents didn't appreciate her tenacity.

Before I'd walked into the shop, I'd wondered if seeing her again would make me realize it had all just been youthful infatuation. Despite how small Rainbow Valley was, I somehow remained out of her orbit. I suspected this was by design on her part.

Now, I realized it hadn't been youthful infatuation at all.

Kate had been it for me and likely always would be.

And then I'd stood before her, ready to deceive.

Deceive her so I could salvage part of our dream.

What a fool I was.

Maybe it was the only way to settle the score between us. Once, she had deceived me. Though I'd learned to hate myself for how I'd treated her that last night, it had been her who had attempted to manipulate my dreams. All because she didn't trust me to come back to her. Couldn't she see that I would have always come back to her?

As I sat in the cafe waiting for her to arrive, I told myself that I'd be happy if she finally lashed out at me for what had happened that night. Maybe that would even things out for us. Part of me wanted her to destroy me.

Maybe I just wanted to burn it all down. I'd convince her to sell that dream of hers and then neither of us would have the dream we'd envisioned all those years ago.

Then I could take that damned house and destroy it myself. No more driving past it and imagining all the little auburn-haired babies running across the yard.

God, I was sick of that. I should let Ted destroy it.

And yet I couldn't.

When Kate walked into the cafe, my stomach flipped. Time hadn't dulled her effect on me. Even in high school, I could remember seeing her walking down the hallway, that bright auburn hair standing out amongst all the other girls. We'd not become a thing until after she'd graduated. Her being a year behind me hadn't offered many opportunities for us to get to know one another.

But it had always been her, even before I'd realized it.

I still wasn't sure how I was going to persuade her to give up the shop. How could I persuade her to sell her dream? Especially now that she was so jaded?

As she took the seat across from me, I cataloged everything about her. Those lush, pouty lips. Eyes that seemed to analyze and take everything in. I'd once seen those eyes lit with a passion only for me.

"You look amazing." Damn. After her cool reception at the shop, I'd planned to be more cautious, less obvious.

And here I was, laying it all out before us.

A blush crept up her cheeks. Although I wished I'd opened with something else, I couldn't resent seeing that I still could make her blush.

"How is your mother?" she asked, picking up the menu and ignoring my compliment. She stared at the menu as if she didn't come into the cafe frequently. Anything to keep her eyes off me.

"She's good. She asks about you all the time."

"She asks you?" Finally, she dared to glance at me over the top of her menu. "Doesn't she realize you'd be the last person to know what's going on with me?"

Ouch.

Kate was never good at masking her feelings.

"Maybe I'd like to answer her questions now and then."

"I don't understand why there's this sudden interest, Matthew." My name from her lips was like a caress. "You haven't said a word to me in ten years. We've gone on with our lives. I know you've had other interests."

Oh, she did, did she?

It was a small town. I'd been semi-serious with Meredith a few years back. She'd probably heard about that through the grapevine. And judging from the way she was looking at me now, it had caused her to hurt.

That she would be jealous fed my ego, but I didn't want to see her hurt. Even with my plan to save the house by convincing her to sell the shop, I was certain it would be the best for both of us in the end.

And surely there had been someone else for her.

Maybe she had someone else now. I grit my teeth, pushing the thought out of my mind.

But if there was someone else, why hadn't I heard about him?

Still, I knew I couldn't completely bullshit Kate. Even at her most innocent, Kate had a decent bullshit detector.

"Ted Palmer has the Richardson estate. He has plans to raze it."

Kate's expression changed from one of cool indifference to one of hurt. She stayed silent for so long that I wondered if she had zoned out completely.

"Why tell me?" Her question came out as barely a whisper. God, how I wanted to reach across the table, take her in my arms and tell her it would all be okay. We could still have that dream together. We'd give Ted what he wanted. Then we could build a new shop for her and the life we'd dreamt of. There were a dozen places more suited to Old Things New, and I'd buy her several if she required it.

"I found out yesterday." I couldn't dwell on the dreams of the past. Not right now. "I didn't want you to drive by one day and see it gone."

"I never drive by." She placed the menu down on the table as Mara Langdon, the proprietor of the cafe, came to take our orders. Mara was a gossip and was much too interested in what was going on at our table.

"Maybe it would be best if it was no longer there," she said after Mara had left. "Maybe..."

The sentence hung in the air, unfinished. I wanted to bed her to finish the thought.

"Can't we at least be friends, Kate?"

"Why?"

"Because I've never stopped missing you."

There. I'd said it. I'd filled most of my days with thoughts of Kate. And now that I'd been near her again, I suspected I'd spend most of my time dwelling on the swell of her hips, the curve of her lips.

"Do you think that's wise, Matthew?"

"I can't be this close to you and not realize how much I miss us being together like this. Talking about everything. Anything. Stupid stuff. Important stuff."

Like dream houses and babies in the yard.

For a minute, she said nothing. I did what I could to salvage the conversation.

"How's your sister?" I asked, determined to keep her talking. Being in real estate, I knew how to talk to people. Knew how to charm them, and get them talking. I hadn't set out to play Kate in this little charade, but I wanted to win this game.

I wanted to win her.

"She's getting married," Kate answered, not completely softening to me, but taking the branch I had extended. "She told me last night. I'm to be the maid-of-honor. She's been texting me non-stop."

"Who's she marrying?"

"Mark Jensen."

Unfortunately, despite the charm I'd acquired from hocking real estate, I couldn't school my face. Fortunately, Kate gave me the first smile she'd given me since she'd walked through the door.

"You know him?"

"It's a small town. It's hard not to know him." Realizing that I was dangerously close to insulting her future brother-in-law, I tried to reel in my thoughts. "There's nothing really wrong with him. He's just not who I expected Cassie to wind up with. He's—"

"Annoying." Kate's smile dazzled me. "He knows everything. There's nothing he doesn't know about and if you mention just about anything, he will tell you all the ways you're wrong about it. Apparently, he knows better than I about how to run my business. And antiques. I'm always so pleased when he stops in so he can tell me about everything I should change about my shop."

"That's him. And don't worry. It's not just you. He accompanied his mother on the inspection of the house she bought last year. Informed me of everything I was doing wrong in real estate and made suggestions to the inspector on how to better do his job."

Kate grimaced and covered her face. "That guy is going to be my brother-in-law. For the rest of my life."

"Well, maybe not. Not that I'd wish divorce on your sister, but I can't imagine Cassie not tiring of that."

"She's completely in love with him. She doesn't see any of his faults. As far as she's concerned, he's right about everything. She might be more convinced of his superiority than he is, which is a feat. But he treats her well. That's the good thing. As long as he's simply annoying and doesn't hurt her, I can live with that."

Neither of us said anything. We both knew what was unspoken. I had hurt her, and she had hurt me. No matter how annoying Mark was, at least he hadn't destroyed the one he was supposed to love.

Something was making the hairs on the back of my neck stand on end. As if someone was staring at us, listening to every word we were saying. Turning, I caught the sight of Mara standing just to the side of the cash counter. While Mara wasn't malicious, she was a well-known gossip. And paying attention to what had once been Rainbow Valley's golden couple would no doubt earn her some juicy gossip.

I sighed. I'd made a mistake by choosing this place, but there was another option. Looking back at Kate, I saw Kate had caught the direction of my gaze. She smiled, knowing as well as I did what a gossip Mara was.

"Could I take you out to dinner this weekend?" I watched as Kate stiffened, but I plowed on. "Somewhere that we could talk and not have someone listening in?"

I spoke the words just a little louder for our audience's benefit. Mara rewarded me with a huff as she disappeared into the kitchen.

"I don't know, Matthew." Despite her words, I could see the wheels turning. She was considering it.

"Just one dinner, Kate. I'll pick you up."

"Do you even know where I live?"

"Yes."

She stared at me, no doubt wondering what else I knew about her current life.

"Alright." Kate sighed. "*A* dinner. That's it. We catch up and then we move on."

I smiled. We would definitely move on.

CHAPTER 5

KATE

I was an idiot.

It'll only be one dinner. Just catch up and then go our separate ways.

Idiot.

Being near him in the cafe told me there would be no "catching up and going our separate ways." It was all bullshit. Being near him reminded me of all the little things about him that had made my heart flutter. The way he smiled that lopsided smile when he was pleased with himself. His hair was always a bit too boyishly haphazard to ever be controlled.

There were more subtle changes as well. I'd missed seeing him grow into the man he had become. Time had chiseled him into a man who exuded confidence. He was always charming, but now his charm was lethal. Matthew King was no longer the young, devil-may-care boy he once was.

Now he was a sexy, charming, devastatingly handsome man who was trying to reassert himself back into my life. And I was doing nothing to stop him. I was stepping right into whatever trap he was setting for me.

I couldn't talk to anyone about this. Sure, I could call Everly, but only Matthew and I knew what our crazy history had been like. I didn't doubt that Everly had heard about our love affair during her time in Rainbow Valley, but it had been one of those "you needed to be there" things.

One dinner date. Maybe if I continued to tell myself that, I'd actually believe it.

We hadn't even had one another's phone numbers. We'd had to exchange numbers as if we hadn't once slept in each other's arms night after night. We'd never had our own place. We'd always snuck into each other's rooms at our parents' houses, clinging to each other for as long as possible before the morning light broke through the window.

Our families all knew. But we all played the ignorance game. If no one talked about it, it wasn't happening. After all, no one wanted to admit to their parents they were having sex in the bedroom with their boyfriend right down the hall.

When Matthew had texted me after our lunch date and asked if The Candelabra, a fancy restaurant in Rainbow Valley, would be okay, I felt that same jolt of excitement I'd felt when he'd first called me when we'd still been teenagers.

I was in danger. Alarm bells were ringing in my head. I knew I should pay attention to them, but I was determined to ignore them.

I could stay on my guard. I could resist whatever temptation he had planned for me. After all, I'd ignored him for ten years.

What was one night?

One night, sitting across from him, looking handsome as hell and charming as sin.

Even at the cafe, I'd wanted to slide next to him, wrap my arms around him and bury my nose in the crook of his neck. I was curious if he smelled the same. He'd always smelled like freshly showered boy back then. I wondered if he wore cologne now. Already, I was comparing him to my last disastrous date, who had smelled like Axe Body Spray with an underlying hint of something not at all enticing.

When Matthew was younger, he'd always been aware of how he presented himself to the world. He enjoyed looking and smelling nice.

It had never been a vain thing. Matthew was always the tallest guy in the room. Had he been rough and brash, it would have been difficult to make others feel comfortable around him. Yet people gravitated toward him. Not only because he looked the part. He was the real deal.

When he wasn't accusing you of doing things you hadn't done, that is.

Checking my reflection in the mirror one last time, I asked myself if I was trying too hard. I didn't want to appear as if I wanted to bed him. Even though I was a fool, my goal was to get in and get out. No funny business.

Matthew King and Kate Cavanaugh were a thing of the past.

Furthermore, I couldn't help but feel like he was up to something. Whether that something was sating his curiosity after all these years or something else, I wasn't sure.

But I'd do my damnedest to be careful with my heart.

At six sharp, I opened my door, and, for the first time in over ten years, Matthew King stood on my doorstep. The doorstep he had greeted me on all those years ago had been my parents, but the feelings hadn't changed. Excitement. Want. Need.

He was dressed in a tailored suit without a tie, the top button of his shirt undone. Beneath the crisp, white fabric, I could spy a patch of dark, curling chest hair. Looking away, I grabbed my purse and attempted to curtail any attempt by him to step into the house. But as soon as I grabbed the handbag, he had stepped inside behind me, surveying the living area.

Matthew knew better than anyone that he could discern as much about my life without him from looking around my house as he could by asking me. He sold houses for a living. Saw daily the memories scattered about a living area as he helped sellers settle into the idea of letting go. So, I watched as he assessed the worth of my life post Matthew.

He looked perfect in my little living room. It looked like he belonged in the room more than I did. Neither of us would be standing in this house if things had gone the way we imagined. We would have been in the house we had planned to share. The one that was soon to be demolished.

He walked over to a group of photographs on the mantle. There were photos of me with my parents, my sister. There were a couple of Everly and I together in the shop. She'd only come into my life within the last two years, but she'd become as close as family to me in that short amount of time.

As he looked over the photos, I wondered if he noticed the years that were missing from the assembled photographs. There were no pictures of that time. Because as much as we had been together those two years, it was unlikely that any photograph had been taken of me that hadn't included him.

When everything had gone sideways, I'd been tempted to throw away every photo that had featured him. And there were plenty. Photos of the two of us. Photos of us with his family and even a few with my own. I was so hurt that just the sight of those photos made my throat constrict and my breathing impaired. I wanted them far away from me so they couldn't hurt me anymore.

In the end, I'd packed them away. So far away that I'd never accidentally happen upon them when I was looking for something.

As I watched him, I wondered what he was thinking about my life minus him. Was he thinking the same thing? That had he not been such a fool, those photos might feature him as well? Might even be photos of our kids?

If I was going to make it through the night, I couldn't keep sliding down the emotional downward spiral I was on. Fixing my shoulders, I watched as he turned back to me. He looked like a man coming up for air.

Then his eyes roamed over me. I went from feeling melancholy to exposed.

"You look amazing, Kate."

Saying "thank you" felt like too much. He'd hear how my voice had gone all husky and needy, and I didn't want to make myself so vulnerable. So, I simply nodded.

As he led me out to his car, I suppressed a whistle. The glossy exterior of the Porsche winked in the streetlights. Of course he'd have a nice, flashy car. He'd always wanted a vehicle that turned heads. I wouldn't let him see me smile, but my stomach flipped at realizing that somewhere inside the man before me was the same boyish dreamer I'd once known.

Once we were in the car, I watched as his fingers enveloped the gear shift. His long fingers encircled the shaft, coaxing the vehicle into drive. I suppressed the desire to sigh. It was easy to remember the feel of those hands on me. He'd always been so damned good with his hands. I tried not to think about how the experience he'd racked up in the years since had likely made him even more devastating.

I pushed the thought aside. Spending the evening imagining all the sex he'd had with other women was a recipe for disaster. No doubt, they were all more experienced than me. If I went down that rabbit hole, I'd soon be wondering how much sexier they were. How much more beautiful they were.

I cleared my throat.

"This isn't a Volkswagen van," I said, letting a smile curve along my lips, likely the first one of the evening. I would have to be careful. Didn't want him getting the wrong idea.

He laughed. "No, it isn't. As I remember it, we were going to take that van from one end of the country to the other. Find every abandoned place we could and explore them."

"Probably kill ourselves." I was doing my damndest to focus on the less savory aspects of that plan rather than the more attractive ones.

In our late teens and twenties, it was as if we had a death wish. There was something about abandoned places that sparked our imaginations. We'd sneak inside with only a flashlight and an unhealthy amount of curiosity. What I wouldn't dwell on was how many times we'd christened each of those places with a rush of hormones and desire. It was a wonder someone hadn't caught us. Even more of a wonder that we hadn't impaled ourselves on some rusty nail. I focused on the image of one of us falling through a weathered floorboard instead of the memory of us once having sex on a creaky old table in an abandoned farmhouse.

At least our consciences were clear. We'd always cleaned up after ourselves and took nothing that didn't belong to us.

Exploring abandoned places had ended when my relationship with Matthew had ended. I wondered if he'd christened any other abandoned places with anyone else since we'd split company.

"For the record," he said, breaking into my thoughts, "I haven't met anyone who enjoyed the whole abandoned thing as much as you did."

Matthew and I had always joked that we could read one another's thoughts. Back then, it had been a sweet thought that we could sense the other's moods. Now, I wasn't too keen on it.

Of course, there had been one time he hadn't been able to read my thoughts. Otherwise, we wouldn't have been in this awkward situation together. Pity that when we had needed that supposed ability the most, it was nowhere to be found.

Pulling into the restaurant's parking lot, he parked and made his way to my side of the car, determined to beat me to the punch. As I put my hand in his, I could feel the warmth shoot up the length of my arm and flood my body. He pulled me against him, and it took every bit of willpower I could muster not to lean right into him. This close, I could smell him. That same clean, masculine scent. No overpowering cologne. Just the familiar scent of Matthew King and damned if it wasn't intoxicating.

Foolishly, I looked up into his eyes and saw that same heat coursing through my veins reflected in his gaze. I pulled away from him, determined not to lose this battle of wills. He offered his arm to me and I reluctantly took it.

Once we were seated, I was at least able to put some distance between us. I might have to endure the sight of him across from me, but at least I couldn't feel the heat of his body.

We began with the banalities of life, staying clear of anything that might be a conversational landmine. He talked about work and his clients. Told silly stories about people we both knew in town and their quest for the perfect house or location for their business.

I talked about the shop. About Everly's quest for true love and her string of bad dates. I talked about Cassie's impending wedding. I even talked about my parents, deftly maneuvering around my disappointment that they weren't as happy about my successes in life as they were about Cassie's upcoming wedding.

For a while, that was good enough.

And then he asked, "Are you happy, Kate?"

I was struck dumb. I felt tears prickle at the back of my eyes and was relieved that I couldn't see the telltale blur of them in my eyes. I wanted to tell him I would have been much happier had he believed me that night. I was tempted to tell him that. Tell him it hadn't been me, but his mother who had been the one to sabotage that dream.

But I couldn't do that to him. Couldn't do that to her.

"I'm as happy as I can be right now."

I could have lied. Could have told him I was ecstatic with my life. In some ways, I was happy with my life. I loved my shop. I had a healthy friendship with Everly. And though my family irritated me, they weren't sabotaging my life, either. They just weren't enthused about it. Big difference.

He would know that I was lying if I said I was completely happy with my life. He knew I loved being in love because he had been the recipient of that love. And as he watched me, I knew he was looking for cracks in the wall I'd built around myself.

"What about you?" I asked, unable to stop myself. If he was going to venture into this territory, there was no reason I couldn't have some answers myself.

"Right now, I'm happier than I've been in a long time."

"At least I was honest with my answer," I snapped.

"That is honest."

"But it also doesn't answer the question."

He sighed. "At times, I'm very happy. I've been more successful in my career than I could have ever dreamt of. I couldn't ask for a better family. We still have family dinners every Thursday night."

I smiled at that, ignoring the pang of hurt that came with the revelation. Once upon a time, I'd been a part of those family dinners. As it was, I hadn't seen his family in nearly ten years. Occasionally, I'd see a glimpse of his little sister online. She'd grown into a beautiful vixen who had garnered a large following online.

The last time I'd been in her presence though had been when she was a grubby little girl who was fascinated with superheroes and video games.

I'd missed so much.

"I don't understand any of this, Matthew." It was tempting to let the rose-tinted nostalgia take over. Let it gloss over the ugliness that had happened that night and the hurt that had followed. "This is all so sudden. I get something is happening with the Richardson Estate, but all this? Showing up at my shop? Taking me out to dinner? It's a lot, Matthew."

"Are you going to tell me you haven't thought about us in the past ten years?" His voice was strained. It reminded me of the day he had finally told me how he felt about me. How he felt like being without me would be like being without oxygen.

So much for that. Somehow, he had kept breathing for ten years without me.

"Don't you ever think about what might have happened if things had gone differently? Have you forgotten about all the dreams we used to have?"

I bit back the retort that I hadn't forgot about those dreams. He'd done a fantastic job of forgetting all about those dreams the night when he'd found it impossible to believe I was telling the truth.

"None of those women you've been with since me have dreams that resemble yours?"

Oh, it was petty, but I couldn't resist.

"No." His answer was so adamant that I had no choice but to believe him. "The reason that none of those women worked out was that none of them were you."

I didn't look away. Didn't give in to the urge to close my eyes and let the emotions that were threatening to take over steamroll over me.

"Kate, tell me you don't sometimes close your eyes and imagine what things would have been like had it all gone differently."

He leaned closer to me. The only thing that kept him from leaning right into me was the expanse of white cloth-covered table between us.

"Maybe we wouldn't be sitting here tonight." His voice was low. "Maybe we'd be at that house, cuddled together, our kids upstairs."

"This is cruel," I whispered, but he didn't stop.

"Or maybe we'd be right here. We'd have left the kids with the sitter. Then we'd come home together and put them to bed. Later, we'd find our way to our own bed and get to the business of making another."

I squeezed my eyes shut, as much to shut out the intensity of his gaze as to hide my own betraying emotions.

Hearing him call for the check, my eyes popped open.

"What are you doing?"

He turned back to me. There was something so primal and unchecked in his expression that I nearly gasped.

"I'm getting us out of here."

CHAPTER 6

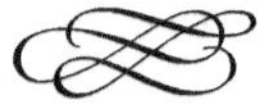

MATTHEW

This wasn't going according to plan.

I had no plan going into this. Nothing other than convincing Kate to give up her dream and, maybe somehow, convince her that the dream we'd once had was better. As if we could just pick up where we left off and be that young, wistful couple all over again.

If she would forgive me when she realized what I'd done.

The conversation had gone off the rails. It had started well enough. All the stupid, inane sort of conversation I had with a client.

Then I had to ask her if she was happy.

I wanted her to be happy, of course. But I also didn't want her to be that happy. Yes, I was selfish. I wanted to know that she had always looked for me in the corners of her life. Wanted to know that it had disappointed her when she hadn't found me there.

Just as I had been.

I wanted her. I wanted to reach over, pull her on top of the table, and take her right there. Claim her so completely that she would consider nothing but being with me forever. Make up for the fact that I hadn't been inside her every night for the past ten years.

Damn her for taking that away from me, from both of us.

I should have been with her that night and all the other nights before. Should have seen all the slight changes to her body that the years had brought about. How many men knew her body better than I did? Damn every one of them straight to hell.

"I'm sorry," I said once we'd settled back into the car. "I didn't mean to start something that would make us so—"

"Emotional?"

"Something like that." More like needy. Desperate. Ripping that dress off her, spreading her legs, and plowing right into her in front of God and everyone sort of desperate.

The gear shift strained beneath the strength of my grip. I wanted to reach across her lap and run my hand up her thigh. She'd worn a flimsy little green dress that fell somewhere between her hips and her knees.

A memory hit me like a freight train. She and I driving to some abandoned place in my shitty Honda. I'd been unable to wait until we got to our destination, so I reached over and pushed my hand between her thighs. I could still hear her breathy pants as I volleyed between keeping us on the road and plunging into her wet heat. When she writhed in the passenger seat, coming apart, I'd been so damned proud of myself.

Yes, I'd been a careless idiot. But God, how I wanted to feel that dampness on my fingers. Bring my fingers to my lips and taste how she tasted now. I was certain that she had grown even sweeter over time, like fine wine.

She was always ready for me. And damned if I didn't believe that she wouldn't be ready for me right then if I'd been bold enough to attempt it.

I was gripping the steering wheel so forcefully that it was a wonder I wasn't leaving indentations on the leather.

My mind was so filled with thoughts of Kate, her breathy moans, her squirming against my hand, that I didn't realize that I'd turned away from the route back to Kate's house and toward another house. Somehow, I'd begun to live in that second timeline scenario that had been floating through my mind. The one where I drove her back to our dream house. The one where the kids we were supposed to have by now would already be asleep in their beds. I'd pay the babysitter and send her on her way. Then I would lead Kate, my wife, upstairs and sink into her, right where I belonged. Maybe I'd put another baby inside her if she'd let me.

"Where are we going?" Kate finally asked. And damn her for asking because I knew she knew.

"I didn't mean to come this way." It was the truth, at least. My brain had gone into some weird alternate history. I could see myself in a parallel universe, driving home with my wife Kate instead of Kate as the skeptical near-stranger next to me. I hated that alternate version of myself for having the one thing I wanted most.

The Richardson estate was located several miles down a long, lonely, winding country road. When we'd used to imagine raising our family here, we'd liked the idea of its proximity to town. There wouldn't be many cars on the street. Even when we'd been nothing more than kids ourselves, we'd been thinking of the welfare of our imaginary family. As I drove along the desolate road, I could hear Kate telling me how we'd not have to worry as much about our kids playing outside. This far from town, there wouldn't be much traffic.

She'd still worry, she had told me. I could even see her face. How wistful she'd looked as she imagined our imaginary babies toddling across the lawn. I'd probably looked a little wistful myself, watching her dreaming of our future. It had been a pretty potent aphrodisiac.

Next to me, Kate clenched her fists into the flimsy fabric of her skirt. I wondered if she was trying to push back the same thoughts that I was having or if she was worried about seeing the place again. Hadn't she told me she no longer drove past it?

"We should be able to see it one last time." I was a liar. A horrible, disgusting liar. This whole ruse had been so that there wouldn't be a last time. Likely, this night would forever have the tinge of deceit. She might hate me for it.

And yet, nothing that could stop me.

Pulling into the drive of the old Victorian, I didn't give a damn about any deceit. Part of me was still angry with that alternate version of me that was getting exactly what he wanted. From the corner of my eye, I watched Kate taking in the sight of the old house. There was a slight intake of breath as we turned toward it. As if all the memories she had suppressed had hit her all at once.

The old Victorian was three stories high, not including the attic. It was accented with the gables and pitched roofs that usually accompanied such an architectural style. Kate had loved it because it looked like something out of a storybook, even with all the cosmetic problems it had acquired. In fact, that was one thing that appealed to her. That it was something that had been forgotten by time, and she was the only person who could adopt it and restore it to its former glory.

There had been a couple who had attempted to rejuvenate it after Kate and I had separated. Before Ted had come to me with his devil's bargain. According to Ted, they'd realized what a money trap the house was and had been willing to part with it as soon as Ted had graced their doorstep. I'd thought the house had sold to someone else, but apparently I'd been mistaken.

Why hadn't I bought the damn thing? Fixed it up and one day picked Kate up from that little antique shop and showed her the fruit of my labors?

Because it wouldn't have been what she wanted. She would have wanted to have been a part of the renovations, the decisions.

And there was also that other thing. She may have rejected me outright, and that would have hurt worse than anything. I may not have been refusing to drive past the old house, but I'd done my best to keep it out of the periphery. Out of sight and out of mind.

If I had bought the house years ago, I wouldn't be doing this right now.

The night air hit my face as I got out of the car. It felt like an admonishment. The best thing to do would be to tell Kate everything that Ted had propositioned me to make her "see reason" on her little dream and to give it up to have our dream.

But I knew as soon as I told her that, this night would be over. I was too selfish to let that happen.

I walked to her side of the car. Kate didn't attempt to get out of the car, staring ahead at the house before looking over at the door as I opened it. Taking her hand, I pulled her from the car, ignoring how good her hand still felt in mine. I didn't relinquish her hand as I led her toward the house and up the steps.

"Do you have a key?" she asked as our feet clomped on the hollow wooden steps as we walked to the front door.

"I'm a real estate agent. There's always a key." Feeling around the frame of the door, I found it where I suspected it would be. Just over the lip of the door frame's edge. Likely, the previous owners were hoping someone would come in and do enough damage to the house to file a decent insurance claim and break even.

"What about cameras?" she asked as I slid the key into the keyhole.

"Ted doesn't care enough about this property to worry about cameras." That should make sense to her. After all, I'd told her he wanted to raze the house. Why would he bother with cameras for a house that would soon be nothing more than kindling?

Furthermore, not long after Ted had come to my office, I'd already driven over and looked the house over. There were no cameras. It seemed as if no one had even stepped foot on the property in years. There was no telling what we might find when we stepped inside. Families of raccoons? Bats hanging from the ceiling? Evidence of satanic rituals conducted in the parlor?

The door opened. There was an unmistakable smell of a building that had been left to fend for itself. The air was stale. There was the slight smell of old wood and something else that wasn't quite identifiable. It wasn't an altogether unpleasant smell, just one that I associated with all things old.

Given that Kate was a connoisseur of all things old, it must have been a familiar scent, if not one that was welcome.

The good thing was that there wasn't a scent of rot. At least nothing had burrowed inside and hadn't been able to find its way out.

In the past, when I'd led her into old, abandoned buildings, there had been a ritual. There was the expectation that we would end the journey with us naked and me inside her. Unfortunately, my body hadn't forgotten that and was already reacting to the possibility.

"It's not changed much," she said as she stepped into the foyer and looked around. The moon was full, giving the rooms an eerie, supernatural glow. It made her look like the ethereal heroine of some gothic novel, looking around an old estate.

"I'm sure you know that someone bought it not so many years ago. Since us." I watched as she flinched at those last two words. It made me feel no better to say them. "They fixed what they could, but it was just too much of a money pit. It's structurally sound, at least."

That I'd made sure of. While I was no contractor, years in the real estate business had given me an eye for when a property was beyond help. The house had good bones and while it would take quite a bit of money to see it to its original glory, the potential was there.

It was more than I could say for most of the places we once ventured into.

"I met the people who bought it some years back. Hated them at the time, but they were decent people." I looked around as I talked, not knowing what I had intended when I led her into the house, only knowing what I had wanted. We'd entered what had likely once been referred to as a parlor. It was a larger room with an ornate fireplace and a large picture window that looked out onto the expansive front porch. It was the kind of room where you had company. Where you unwrapped Christmas gifts with your family. Where you invited people over to celebrate a new job or introduce a new baby.

"They'd had some idea that it was going to be this ongoing project house. They'd likely watched a bit too much HGTV. Retired couple. It was too much for them, but they managed some stuff before they checked out. They got the staircase up to code and…"

Turning to face her, I could see the moonlight glinting off her cheeks. Wet streaks were cascading from her eyes down to her chin. She'd been crying. She'd likely started when I'd been rambling on about the former owners and I'd completely missed her distress

"Kate." I stepped to her and then stopped, unsure what I should do. She was so close, I could feel the heat of her body.

"It's fine, Matthew. It's fine." She brushed aside a tear and I could tell it was nothing close to fine. I'd once been so good at reading her moods, anticipating when she was about to cry or get angry. And now, enough time had passed where I was completely oblivious to her being in distress.

"It's not fine." The words came out a little more forcefully than I had intended, and she flinched. "And it hasn't been fine for a long time and we both know it."

It happened so quickly that I was certain there had been no thought process from the time I'd stopped speaking until I had my arms around her. I brought her to me, relishing the feel of her body against mine. Resting my chin atop her head, I swayed slightly.

"I'm an asshole for bringing you here." I was an asshole for so many things that if I went down the list with her now, she would push me away so forcefully I would fall right through the questionable floor beneath me.

"I'm an asshole for a lot of things," I said finally. Pulling back, I looked down at her.

Then I leaned forward and brushed my lips against hers. It was just skin against skin, her soft lips surrendering to my own. That soft brush hit me with such a feeling of desire, nostalgia, and need that I couldn't resist deepening the kiss. She felt so good in my arms, warm, tender, and pliant. She wasn't pushing me away. In fact, she was eagerly plundering my mouth, tasting, licking, nibbling. A little moan escaped her and it was like she had injected fire into my veins. My cock stiffened, aching to find its home inside her. Her hands found my chest, rubbing and pulling at the fabric of the shirt beneath my jacket.

My mouth left hers as I blazed a trail of kisses from the line of her jaw to the curve of her neck.

"Matthew?" Her voice sounded strained and needy, yet deep and sultry. It was the voice of a woman who wanted exactly what I wanted as badly as I did.

"Yes." I didn't know what question I was answering, but it seemed like the most honest answer. Because yes, this is exactly what we should do tonight. Only the house shouldn't be a bare husk. It should have been filled with furniture that we'd picked out. There should be night lights in the kids' rooms and all those little sounds that we'd grown used to over the years. We should be upstairs in our shared bedroom, where I would place her on a bed that was soft and familiar. A bed where we'd made all our babies and hopefully more.

This wasn't the best solution for reunion sex, but my need for her was too great to put a stop to it. I drew away from her just enough to rip the jacket from my body, throwing it down on the floor below us. She glanced down at the garment and then up at me before she sunk to the satiny inner lining of the jacket and pulled me down with her.

I wanted to taste every inch of her. Pull her nipples into my mouth and suck them until she cried out my name over and over again, but I needed her too much. I needed to taste her. That desire to sink my fingers into her and taste her in the car was still hot in my mind. Reaching up beyond the hem of her skirt, I ripped the panties from her and gazed down at the glistening sight of her.

I ran one finger up her slit and she rewarded me with a sound that seemed like a cross between a moan and a sigh. Like someone who had finally found relief from a pain that had haunted her for much too long.

"You're so wet, Kate. You were always so wet for me."

And just like I'd imagined in the car, I brought my fingers to my lips and tasted her. That sweet tangy bliss of her nectar was like giving a nibble to an addict. Bending down, I brought my lips to hers and tasted her. She was soaked, and I was drinking of her as if I would never get enough.

Because I never would.

Pushing her legs farther apart, I drew her quivering clit into my mouth and sucked and licked until she bucked against me. She was panting, gasping for breath, moaning as her pussy trembled. I pushed a finger into her and let her muscles grasp and tug at me as I sunk two more into her. She was still so tight. Still so made for me.

She moaned, long and low, as she clenched around my finger and drenched me. My god, she was magnificent.

"Now, Matthew." She was writhing, begging, as I pulled my lips away from her and looked over her body. I pulled myself up, looking down at the beautiful woman beneath me. She'd never looked more beautiful, with her hair wild around her and her chest heaving. Her hand reached out, clamoring for me.

I would have her in this house, finally. If only for tonight, Kate Cavanaugh would belong to me.

CHAPTER 7

This should feel wrong. Matthew King had only appeared back in my life less than 24 hours ago and now he was between my legs, his lips around my clit.

But I needed him. I'd needed him for so long that it didn't occur to me to ask questions. I didn't want to stop. Didn't want to think that this might be a bad idea. I still didn't know why he had shown up at the store. The claim that Ted Palmer was buying the Richardson Estate was a little too neat and clean for me.

But God. There was no feeling like the feeling of Matthew between my legs. He had been the only one. I'd known the minute he had first touched me all those years ago that there would be no one else who could touch me like he could. I'd dreamt of him inside me every night since we'd been apart. This might not have been how I had imagined us coming together once again, but I refused to be picky when I was finally getting exactly what I wanted. I'd be damned if I was about to put a halt to it because the location wasn't ideal.

"Now, Matthew." My voice was breathy, needy, foreign to me.

He moved to hover over me. He looked incredible. Breathless, wild. His hair stood on end, wild and untamed. The moonlight from the windows gave him an otherworldly appearance. Matthew King, a ghost of the past, here to ravish me.

"I didn't bring anything, Kate."

I was hovering between panic and annoyance. Panic that this was where this would end. Annoyance that he hadn't set out to seduce me.

But I didn't want this to end. If he didn't want to risk this with me after all these years, wouldn't it mean that tonight had been a whim and he had no intention of this going any further?

"Are you okay with that, darling?"

My stomach flipped at the endearment. The reality of what we were about to risk made the moment even more fraught with tension. I shouldn't be okay with this. I should act responsibly. I shouldn't take this risk.

But this was what I had wanted for the last ten years. And if this was the only way I'd get it, by God, I was going to take it.

"Yes, Matthew. This is what I want."

I reached up, pulling his shirt from him. He was more broad, toned, and defined than he had been the last time I'd seen him. It was the sculpted body that came from pushing a body to its limit. It was the body of a man designed to be touched and loved. I cursed every woman who had loved this version of Matthew's body.

As he pulled my dress over my head and removed that final layer of fabric that hid my body from his view, a new panic washed over me. Over the years, he had grown only more defined, cut. The years had softened me. There were curves where there hadn't been curves before. Was he still expecting that same young girl with stick-thin limbs and bony hips? I'd given up on ever finding her again, but had he?

He stopped, looking down at me, and I swallowed, fearing that I'd disappointed him. Whereas the changes to his body excited me, there was the real possibility that my body did the exact opposite.

"Every dream I've had of us together, none has done you justice," he said as he ran his hand down the slope of my breast and across the curve of my hip. Such a simple touch, yet it made me shiver.

"You're not disappointed?" The question embarrassed me. My

insecurities swam in my mind constantly, but typically I did a decent job of keeping them confined there.

"Disappointed?" He almost sounded offended. "Kate, you're a goddess. I never want to stop touching you."

"Then don't." It was a command, but it felt more like begging. Because I didn't want him to stop touching me. Being without him again might be the end of me.

He lowered his lips to my neck, kissing a trail to my breast. He took a taut nipple between his lips and suckled. I gasped at the sensation. The warmth of his lips surrounding me, the satin lining of his jacket beneath me. It all created a strange, erotic sensation that made the whole thing feel unreal. I couldn't get close enough to him. I arched into him, begging him to take more of me. When he'd suckled one breast to the point it was swollen and aching, he moved to the next. He took it into his mouth, determined to lavish the same amount of attention on it as the previous.

My legs spread wider, beckoning him in. He was still clothed from the waist down, but I could feel his erection beneath the fabric of his pants. Reaching down, I fumbled with his belt until he finally left my breast long enough to help me. Our fingers tangled as we pushed the fabric over his hips and his cock sprang forth, eager to join with me.

Running my hand down his length, he rewarded me with a low moan. It was a sound I had dreamt of for years. Low, masculine, and desperate. A sound that told me he needed more and would do what he had to in order to scratch that itch.

"Kate." It was just one word. It was a name I heard countless times throughout the day. But on his lips, my name was like a benediction. The way he said it made it sound as if a thousand other words were hiding behind it. I ran my thumb over his tip, rewarded with the slickness that seeped from the tip. He jerked and his tip grazed my entrance, making it my turn to groan in frustration. He moved his hips, making the length of his cock kiss my slit.

His gaze looked down to where the two of us were nearly joined, and I followed, looking down as he rubbed himself against me. I was so slick, he glided across me easily. The view was intoxicating. His long, thick shaft rubbing eagerly against me. He looked up at me, his eyes finding mine.

"You're certain, my love?"

I nodded, letting out a low, breathy "yes," and he reached down, positioning himself. He pushed in slowly, nestling the tip between my eager lips. He met the familiar resistance that always accompanied our lovemaking. He was so large, I hugged him like a glove. It had been a while, and I'd grown unaccustomed to the feel of his girth.

"So tight," he breathed, closing his eyes as he pushed into me. He was taking his time, determined not to hurt me. I stretched around him, feeling that aching, longing burn I'd needed for so long. I bucked up into him, letting him know it was okay to thrust harder, faster, and further.

It was a dance that we had once been familiar with and we fell back into it like it had been only days and not years since we had last met like this.

I wanted all of him, needed to feel his length press up against that innermost wall. When he finally bottomed out inside me, I let out a whoosh of breath. Finally, he was where I wanted him. I closed my eyes long enough to allow myself to relish how he felt inside me.

"I'd only been able to dream of how right this felt." I opened my eyes, staring up at him. I was startled by how intense his expression was as he stared down at me. "You were made for me, Kate."

He drew back and plunged into me. My breath left me. He moved in and out of me, never taking his eyes from my face as our bodies mingled. Our bodies were slick with sweat. The warm summer evening and our bodies moving together made the heat between us spark like kindling.

I spread my legs wider, trying to take in as much of him as possible as his thrusts grew wilder and his rhythm became quicker.

Our bodies slapped together, echoing inside the empty house. Grunts, moans, and pants between us made a primal soundtrack for the moment we were creating.

His hands went beneath my knees, bringing them up and angling me so that he could thrust deeper and harder.

"Matthew, oh Matthew." They were the only coherent words I could manage, but they seemed to work like magic on the man who was thrusting inside me. His name on my lips urged him on as if I'd spoken a sort of secret incantation that drove him to the brink of insanity.

My hands went to his back, my fingernails digging into the taut, toned flesh. His hips bucked into me. The slapping sensation of each thrust met with a wet burst of desire as that innermost part of me grasped at him. The jacket beneath us slid with us as he pounded into me. As all those sensations sparked inside me, my eyelids grew heavy. I was tempted to close my eyes and ride that little earthquake, but I wanted to watch his face as he came.

He was moaning, panting, his hair falling across his forehead as he pushed us both to our limits. Reaching down between us, his fingers grazed my clit. Shockwaves of pleasure surged through my body as my orgasm hit. I closed my eyes, unable to resist the pull of my release.

But I wanted to watch him. The twist and pull and quivering of my pussy tore a shout from me as he plunged into me over and over again. As he jerked and lost his rhythm, I felt that delicious heat as he flooded me. I pulled my legs around him, imprisoning him inside me, determined to take every ounce of him within me.

"Kate." He rested his forehead against mine as he regained control of his breathing. "Kate."

There were so many things I wanted to say. I wanted to make him promise not to leave me again. To stay inside me right where he was until he grew hard again and then take me as relentlessly as he had just done.

I didn't give a damn about the house. All I wanted was him inside me. His intoxicating weight over me as he fought to gain control. His expression was that of a man who had found completion. No matter what happened after this night, I would remember that expression. The one that told me he had found what he was looking for inside me and that, I hoped, he would never find it again inside anyone else.

Finally, unable to hold himself aloft any longer, he pulled out of me and the sensation was both gratifying and devastating. I clamped my legs around him as he rolled over, determined to keep what I could of him inside me. It was ridiculous to think that the one time we had finally been together would create life within me. I was fairly certain I wasn't ovulating.

But that didn't stop me from thinking about those old dreams and how much I'd wanted that family we had dreamt of together.

He rolled over beside me, his back meeting with the bare hardwood of the floor beyond the edge of his jacket that had served as our bed. I worried he would jump to his feet as soon as he regained control of himself and the night would be over. Instead, he reached out and pulled me to his chest. I sighed. It was the same way we'd fallen together when we had been younger. My head against his chest, listening to his heartbeat slow from the wild, erratic beat that had been the music of our lovemaking.

"How the hell have I managed without you?" he asked, and if his heartbeat was slowing at that moment, mine was soaring into the stratosphere.

"Don't throw me away again." I hadn't meant to say the words out loud. I'd meant for them to stay in the back of my mind along with all my other silent demands.

Don't let this end. Let him stay inside me. Let this be a beginning.

Beneath me, he pulled away, and for a minute, I was afraid I'd said the wrong thing. That this was the moment he would finally reject me and turn me out, but instead, he hovered above me, staring down at me.

His eyes looked over me, seeming to take inventory of every plane of my face.

"Did you think of me?" he asked, his voice deep and low, the sound of it almost palpable like a phantom caress. He brought his hand down, sliding over the slick planes of my body.

"When you touched yourself right here," his hand came between my thighs, coaxing them open from the tight fortress I'd made to dam his seed inside me, "did you see me? Did you say my name as you made yourself come?"

I groaned, bucking against his hand.

"Yes, Matthew." It wasn't a lie. Not one damn night had gone by when I didn't think of Matthew King.

"Show me," he commanded and removed his hand. I considered reaching down and showing him exactly what he had been missing. My fingers hovered above that sated area of myself that grew hungry for him again.

"No."

At first, he looked surprised, and then that devilish smile slid across his lips.

"No, Kate?"

"No, Matthew." I sounded desperate. Determined. "It's like you said. I spent many a night touching myself and wishing it was your hand instead of mine. You make me come, Matthew. You."

His expression changed. There was something possessive about the way he looked down at me. His fingers returned to me, his hand pushing my legs wide as he looked once more at my face, and then his gaze traveled down to where his hand toyed with me.

It took only seconds, his hand playing me expertly before I was jerking and thrusting into his movements. Sitting up slightly as I came down from my release, his hands roughly grasped my hips and turned me onto my stomach.

"On your knees, Kate." It was a forceful command that made my nipples peak in anticipation. Wobbly though I was, I brought myself to my knees and groaned as I felt his thickness, as hard as granite, grazing that well-used part of me.

Impaling me on him, I shouted as he filled me. I was still tight and wet. My pussy was so sensitive that my body shook as his head met that final resistance inside me. As he pumped in and out of me, I was no longer aware of the building around us. Just him, moving in and out of me as my fingers dug into the silk lining of Matthew's jacket. The sounds of his grunts and pants, the sporadic crying out of my name, seemed to be in some far-off room as a violent release began to overtake me. It was harsh, long, and overpowering. A full body release that made my legs shake, my arms wobble, and that sheath that held him clamp at his intrusion. I knew he could feel that squeeze of muscles as he cried out. This time, I could barely register the moment he spent himself inside me. Unable to register the emotions that my release had brought with it.

There were tears on my cheeks as he gathered me to him. He maneuvered me so I was on top of him and held me, shaking, to his quivering body.

I didn't realize that I was saying anything until my body began to descend from the rapid ascent of our bliss.

"Don't leave me again," I said, my brain on hiatus as my body took over every part of my thought process. The words were choked, and I was embarrassed to realize that tears were bathing Matthew's chest. He was cooing, shushing me, his hand in my hair, caressing me as he held me to him.

As I grew quieter, embarrassed by my outburst, his chest rumbled beneath me as he finally spoke.

"I'm sorry, my love. I'm so sorry. I'll never let you go again."

CHAPTER 8

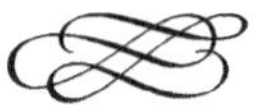

KATE

It was one night, but it seemed like the entire world had brightened within just the few hours that Matthew and I had spent together. It was as if a dark cloud hanging over my life had suddenly disappeared.

But now? Now it was gone. And I felt all those ridiculous things I'd felt the first time Matthew finally noticed me.

I felt like someone in love.

"Good morning, Everly!"

Everly looked up from the computer. She was standing behind the counter, no doubt prepping the day's social media posts and replying to messages. Her glasses balanced on the end of her nose. The ensemble gave her a "hot for teacher" look that would drive men wild if she'd bother to give even one of them a chance.

She was staring at me as if she didn't recognize me. I stopped.

"What? Is something wrong with my outfit?" I looked down at my clothes. Jeans and an off-the-shoulder top that dangled over a tank top. It was comfortable, yet stylish and, after my night with Matthew, I wanted to show off my figure a bit. All the things he'd said about my body. The way his hands slid over my curves. It was as if he'd marked me and I could still sense that burning trail beneath the fabric of my clothes.

"Holy shit, Kate." Everly pulled off her glasses and made her way around the counter. She circled me like a fashion guru in some sort of fashion TV reality series. I didn't think my choice of outfit was all that different from my usual fare, but perhaps I was showing off a little more curves than usual?

"You got laid last night!"

I looked around, expecting a customer to pop out from around a shelf. Then I remembered the store was still closed.

And yet, despite my momentary embarrassment at having been found out, I couldn't stop the goofy smile that stretched my lips.

Everly circled before me once again, looking at me seriously, and then her eyes grew wide.

"No way."

"What?" I was trying to figure out what else she'd discerned from circling me. Everly had a finely tuned understanding of human nature. It was what made her so good at the social media stuff. She understood what people would respond to and what they would ignore. She could be the head of a Fortune 500 company someday if she wanted to.

"You didn't just get laid, Kate. You're in love."

See?

There was no point in denying it. Especially not to Everly. She was not only a student of the human condition but also a romantic. She'd cultivated an inflated sense of the idea of being in love, which was the reason I figured she'd never been in a relationship for more than a few weeks. Nobody ever stacked up.

There was also no point in denying it because I knew I'd never stopped being in love with Matthew. It wasn't as if we'd shared one night of passion and then I'd fallen head over heels in love with him. We had a history. A history that once included both of us being crazy about each other. Planning a life together. Once upon a time, we'd been each other's forever person.

Shaking my head, I made my way toward the back of the store and into the office.

"The truth is, Everly, I'm terrified," I said as I stepped into the office and threw my handbag into the drawer of my desk. Everly was following close behind, wanting details. It was hard to fault her. For the three years she'd worked for me, we'd become close friends. Not being close to my sister, Everly was as close to the relationship I'd wanted with my sister as I could get without being blood-related.

In the time that Everly had known me, she'd not seen me with anyone romantically. I used to berate myself for not being interested in anyone. After being with Matthew the night before, I understood why I'd been unable to find anyone. He'd given me a high standard to match.

I still didn't know what was happening, and the uncertainty terrified me.

Settling in the chair behind the desk, I looked up at Everly as she propped herself on the edge of the desk. She wanted the details. And strangely, I didn't want to be coy about it either.

"What if something goes wrong?" I asked her.

"What if something goes right?" Everly returned.

I'd never explained my relationship with Matthew to Everly. Rainbow Valley was a small town. Matthew had made a name for himself as a charming yet shrewd businessman when it came to real estate in the area. His charm, plus his dashing good looks, put him high on the list of men who attracted female interest in town. Most people knew about his love life, past and current.

That meant that there was a certain interest in me by proxy. Everly knew Matthew and I had once been an item. She'd also been in the shop when he'd come in. She'd done the math as to who it was who'd put the spring in my step.

"Well, tell me all about it, Kate. I want to live vicariously through you."

I gave her the abbreviated version of the events. Just enough to appease her while keeping the more juicy nuggets to myself.

After Matthew and I had made love, he'd held me to him right there on the floor of the house we'd once dreamt would be ours. We'd talked as if no time had passed. Talked about how we would change the house to our whims if given the chance. Talked about imaginary vacations. How we would pay a housesitter while we were away. We'd mused that my sister would bring over her brood at some point and want us to babysit them. We'd have holidays and parties where we'd invite the whole family. There would be summer BBQs. We even imagined having birthday parties for our imaginary kids.

And just as it had been when we were 19 and 21 instead of 29 and 31, my stomach flipped each time he'd dared to invoke the idea of us having children. As I'd curled up against his bare chest, I'd believed it was all possible. And when he'd lavished me with kisses once more, I'd topped him, riding him to completion this time until he once again spilled inside me.

I knew it was unlikely that we'd already started that family we'd dreamt about. After all, how long had some of my acquaintances tried for their babies before they'd finally gotten pregnant? Still, even the slightest possibility that I might be pregnant made my blood run hot.

In the morning light, however, I knew I wanted more time. Time for us to rebuild all we had lost. I didn't relish the idea of walking down the aisle with a baby bump. Mentally, I kicked myself for planning a wedding that I didn't know would ever happen. Just because Matthew had been adamant about that future didn't mean he was still so keen on it. The things said in the afterglow last night would be best relegated to pillow talk.

Everly sighed as she walked back onto the sales floor. Meanwhile, I laughed at myself for already marrying Matthew in my mind.

Marriage. The thought brought me hurtling back to earth. I was certain I had missed thousands of texts from Cassie and my mother. Once I'd stepped out into the night air with Matthew, I'd turned off the phone. I hadn't bothered to think about it again until now.

As I suspected, the phone was filled with messages from my sister and mother. There was also a text from the man who'd filled my mind pretty much every second since we'd parted company the night before. My stomach flipped at the sight of his name. He was getting some work done at the office on Sunday and wondered if I might be in the mood to meet him at the office for lunch. Matthew had sent the text a few hours ago. I worried he might think I was ignoring him. Would he think I'd changed my mind about the things we'd discussed the night before?

The thought was so ridiculous. I couldn't help but think it would be just as ridiculous to him.

Texting him back that I'd meet him later, I then scrolled through the other messages, seeing only one other that wasn't from Cassie or Mom. It was from Shirlee Conlee asking me to hop over to her shop next door at my earliest convenience. Shirlee was the owner of Things Left Unsaid, a popular stationery store in the little strip of stores that also housed Old Things New. Shirlee had long ago taken it upon herself to know everything that was happening in the town business-wise. As gossip went, it was the most useful sort of gossip one could trade in.

Sunday mornings were only slightly slower in traffic than the rest of the weekend. People were heading back home and usually looking for one more stop in town before they made their way back to their own reality. Even with the steady flow of customers, my mind kept wandering. In every corner of the shop, I saw something that reminded me of Matthew. My heart fluttered with the anticipation of our meeting later in the day. By the time noon hit, Everly shooed me out of the door a few minutes before, so I could stop over at Shirlee's before heading over to Matthew's office.

Things Left Unsaid smelled of crisp, warm linen paper. Just step-ping into the store, my hand itched to pick up one of the fountain pens on display and try my hand at writing an old, rambling journal entry. Customers crowded the shop as I stepped in. I found Shirlee wrapping up a purchase for a couple who'd been in my shop only moments earlier. I smiled at them as they left the store. Shirlee saw me and jerked her head toward the back.

"I wanted to give you a head's up," Shirlee began as she stepped into her office and I took a seat in the chair opposite hers. Shirlee ran a tight ship and her office reflected that. Unlike my own, there was no clutter. No stack of invoices or catalogs that needed organizing. That same need for structure bled into socializing during business hours. She'd keep the visit brief. A good thing since I was eager to get to Matthew.

"Ted Palmer is sniffing around the shops again. It looks like he's going to try to win over the business owners to sell to him. If one of us falls, they may as well all fall. Once he gets a foothold in this place, he'll pressure us until we all fall like dominoes. Hell, he'd paint the storefront he bought neon green just to get us all to move out as soon as possible."

Uneasiness crept up my spine. Before this weekend, I'd paid little attention to Ted Palmer in years. At one time, he'd an unhealthy interest in buying the shops. Just like with the Richardson Estate, he intended to raze them to the ground. His long-term plans to put a development on the land had been thwarted by the shop owners' refusal to sell. All the shop owners had held firm. The weakest link was Grady, the man who'd owned my shop before I'd purchased it. Ted had known he wanted out. He was getting older, and the shop was becoming more of an albatross than a joy to run as it'd been for him in years prior.

It was because of Ted's pressuring him that Grady had come to me with an offer that I couldn't refuse. I'd raised enough to put down on the shop and bought it out from under Ted, a move that Ted had never forgotten and never forgiven. But it at least looked like he'd moved on. Some part of me wondered if his interest in the Richardson Estate hadn't been a late-coming middle finger pointed my way.

It had to be a coincidence. Stranger things happened. I wasn't going to let the little twinge of discomfort in my belly ruin a pleasant afternoon with Matthew.

"Nobody's approached me." I mentioned nothing to her about the Richardson Estate. Likely, it was only a coincidence that he was sniffing around there at the same time as well. "But I know how to deal with Ted. He doesn't scare me."

"I don't think you'll be hearing from Ted, Kate." Dread settled over me and I had the hysterical urge to jump out of my seat and run out of the office and back into the sunshine. Whatever she was about to say, I knew I didn't want to hear it. "It's more likely that you'll be hearing from Matthew King."

And just like that, the weight in my chest dropped into the pit of my stomach. My stomach roiled. There had to be an explanation.

"Matthew King?" My voice sounded high and strained. Bells were clanging in my head. I resisted the urge to massage away the headache blooming in my skull.

"I know you two were close at one time." Shirlee's voice disappeared amid the alarm bells ringing in my head. "But I know that's been a while ago and things have likely changed. I've always heard Matthew is an above-the-table businessman, and he has scruples, but there's a chance that Ted is using him. Likely, he's going to convince Matthew to approach you."

"How do you know Matthew's involved?"

Shirlee smiled a slick, knowing smile. "Kate, you know I keep abreast of all the gossip that goes on in this town for this very reason. I try to keep up with everything, though I do occasionally miss some things. I know Ted has been seen at Matthew's office lately and they usually try to avoid one another.

"I also know that he was in your store the other day."

Shirlee wasn't being cruel. Just factual, but it still felt like a slap.

Surely, everything that had happened between us couldn't have been a ruse to get me to sell the shop. Matthew knew what Old Things New meant to me. I couldn't believe he would be involved in a scheme to convince me to sell the shop.

Last night, he'd told me he would never let me go again. Could he have lied so sweetly? Was he so far past our history that he could use me in such a way?

The world wavered around me. The sweet promise of seeing Matthew in a short while no longer held the same allure that it had before. Now, it seemed like a death march. The final nail in the coffin in our relationship. That final nail that had never been nailed in all those years before was about to finally be hammered in.

"Kate, are you okay?" Shirlee's voice brought me back to the present.

"I'm fine." If ever I'd told a lie, that was likely the greatest one. "You're the best. Thank you for bringing this to my attention. You don't know how much you've helped me out today."

I rose, feeling like the world might move on without me if I moved too quickly. Shirlee rose with me and I could see the worry on her face. She might be shrewd and no-nonsense, but I knew she could be a decent person. If I told her she had shattered my well-being, she would put everything on hold and try to fix what she could.

"It's what I do," she said. She reached her hand out as if she wanted to reach for me, perhaps to steady me or perhaps to make sure I wouldn't disappear into vapor. For a split second, I wished that were possible. How nice would it be to disappear into the ether of the world around me and leave this sinking feeling behind?

Muscle memory carried me through the shop and toward the front door. Shirlee was on my heels. The world seemed shaky and unreal. If I let my mind grasp the realities of what I'd been told, I knew I would collapse right there in the middle of all of Shirlee's customers and bawl my eyes out.

I had to make my way out of the store in one piece. And I had to make my way to Matthew King's office to have a conversation with him for one last time. The thought made me sick, but there was no alternative at this point. Although I hadn't yet talked to him, I knew what I was going to find out. It had all seemed too good to be true. I'd fallen back on my love for him and let him hoodwink me.

I might never get over him, but I wouldn't let him get one over on me. Not again.

"Kate." Shirlee's voice stopped me as I pulled the door open and the entry bell rang overhead. It somehow seemed to pull me back to reality. "Are you sure you're going to be okay?"

Turning back to her, I nodded. "I'll be fine."

I turned and walked out the door and toward my car.

It was a lie, though. I would never be fine again.

MATTHEW

My real estate office was unassuming. Welcoming. A place where my clients were comfortable, but also a place I didn't mind spending a lot of time in as well. The office had once been a Craftsman-style house, an architectural jewel in the Wright-style. It almost seemed out of place among the other unassuming houses in Rainbow Valley.

The town had nearly razed it, but I'd bought it and turned it into a cozy location where clients could dream. It was also a place where I routinely sought some peace and quiet.

And right now, that peace and quiet was being threatened as I watched Ted Palmer walk through the office doors on a Sunday afternoon. It was an off day, but there were some things I needed to get done. I'd hoped to have some time alone to clear my head before I met Kate for lunch.

The evening with Kate had been phenomenal. If there was any doubt that the heat and fire we'd experienced together years ago was still there, we had squelched it in a flurry of caresses and touches. Touches that, despite bringing us to completion multiple times, only made me want her that much more. I knew I'd live my entire life and never get my fill of Kate Cavanaugh.

And I was happy again. While I hadn't spent the last ten years of my life in misery, something was missing. Part of me knew what was missing was Kate. I no longer cared about the stupid school acceptance letter. I only cared about Kate.

In one evening, my life had done a 180.

Seeing Ted in my office only reminded me that my reunion with Kate was predicated on a lie. My gut twisted as I thought of how I hadn't been completely honest with her. Perhaps, in the beginning, I'd wanted to lie to her. To give her a taste of her own medicine.

Then I was standing before her and I only wanted to be with her. Screw the past. I wanted a future with Kate. The next time I saw her, I needed to tell her the truth. I'd tell her everything. Tell her it had always been in the back of my mind to make that dream of ours work.

Because that was the truth.

I only hoped she would understand.

If we lost the house - if Ted made good on his threat and razed it - we would be fine. I'd build Kate another house. A better one.

"Did you make headway with the girl?" Ted asked as he stepped into my office. He had a knack for treating any place he stepped into as if it belonged to him. The way he referred to Kate as "the girl" set my teeth on edge. It was dismissive. Kate was all woman.

"I've spoken with her." I wasn't giving Ted anything he could use against me or Kate. "But here's my question: what makes you think I can convince her to sell the shop to you?"

Ted let out a dramatic sigh. He reminded me of a patriarch from one of the daytime soaps my grandmother watched when I was a kid. He could charm most people out of their life savings. His good looks didn't hurt. My sister, had she not hated the man, might have referred to him as a silver fox.

"I should have known you'd get near her and wouldn't be able to get the job done. You get close to her and your brain drops right into your ballsac."

"Again, why do you think she'd sell? Why focus on her? Why not focus on the other shop owners? Surely there's at least one person there with more capital who wouldn't mind a new storefront."

"That should have been obvious. It's because Kate Cavanaugh is the weakest, Matthew."

My chair nearly tumbled backward as I rose swiftly. It righted itself before it tumbled to the ground. There were a thousand things I wanted to say to Ted. More than anything, I wanted to see what his face would look like when I shoved my fist against his nose.

I wanted to tell Ted all the reasons he was wrong. Kate was far from weak. Ted never had to rely on the strength of will like Kate did. She'd dealt with absent, or worse, critical parents. She'd dealt with me turning my back on her. She'd built her business from the ground up without help from anyone.

And that last still bothered me. I should have been there to help her, and I wasn't. The frustration was more fuel to the fire of my desire to want to rearrange Ted's face.

Ted held up his hands in mock surrender.

"She's the weakest because you're her weakness," Ted explained. "Everyone knows that you never got over one another. It's one of those small-town love stories everyone loves to talk about. Tragic. Star-crossed lovers make for great gossip, Matthew. I always pay attention to gossip. As successful as you are in Rainbow Valley, I thought you would have learned that you should, too."

Right then, what I wanted was Ted Palmer out of my office. I'd never cared for the man, but I couldn't remember a time when the sight of him made me sick, as it did now.

"Honestly, I thought you'd moved on," he continued, much to my annoyance. "You seemed to. While she seems stuck in some sort of relationship limbo, we all know you've moved on. Or at least I assumed you had. But it appears I was wrong.

"Look, it's not just the Richardson Estate. I have too much riding on this. If no one sells, I'm going to have to make things difficult for them."

I tensed, but I was determined not to let the worry and fear that was taking over show. I'd already let him rile me.

"That sounds like a threat, Ted."

He shrugged. "It's not a threat. It's business. Everything I do will be legal, I promise you that. As I said, it's just business."

Ted rose from his seat, smiling as if we'd been doing nothing more than discussing football or the weather.

"Just convince the girl to sell, Matthew. Easy peasy."

He turned, me hot on his heels as I followed him through the lobby. I was determined to see him vanquished out of the building as soon as possible.

As Ted opened the door, Kate stood on the other side of the threshold, looking up at Ted. For a moment, the two of them just stared at each other before Ted smiled his charming snake smile. Giving her a nod, he shot a quick look my way and then disappeared out the door.

Kate didn't turn to watch him leave. Her eyes cut to the side as the door closed behind Ted, leaving us in the lobby. When the door was closed, her eyes returned to me.

Stepping toward Kate, I bent to kiss her, only to have her pull away. She pushed her back against the door.

"You're early," I said. Of all the ridiculous things I could have said. I cursed myself for being so damned obvious. But I didn't know what to say. All I knew was something was wrong, and I knew exactly what that thing was.

"And you're a liar."

The dread that hovered over me ever since Ted walked into my office turned into a leaden weight in my stomach. I wanted to close the distance between us. Pull her to me. Explain everything. Make her understand.

"Interesting seeing Ted in your office. Does he usually come to your office on a Sunday, Matthew?"

Somehow, she'd figured it out. I didn't know how, but the opportunity I'd had to tell her everything had passed. A frantic sensation took over my body. It was as if all my tendons and bones were pulling apart all at once. I was desperate to do anything to make this situation right. If only I could turn back the clock.

"What are you two cooking up together?" She almost looked

desperate. As if she would let herself believe anything if I could only make it sound believable enough. For a second, I considered making up a lie.

In the end, I couldn't.

"Kate…"

"Is this punishment?"

"What?"

"Are you punishing me?" Her voice cracked just a little on the word 'punishment' and God, how I wanted to reach forward and wrap her in my arms. Tell her I was sorry for being such an idiot and promise to do everything in my power to make it okay again. "Are you punishing me for what you believe I did to you all those years ago?"

"I'm over that, Kate. I may not agree with it, but I understand why you did it." I stepped forward, my arm out, desperate to just touch her, but she maneuvered to the side before my hand brushed against her.

I now understood why she'd deleted that email. To have something so precious to you stand before you and threaten to take itself away from you? It made me feel crazy. Is this what she'd felt when I hadn't believed her?

If it was, I couldn't blame her for anything she did.

Kate laughed. It was a hollow, foreign sound that sounded nothing like my Kate. My blood ran cold.

"All these years and you still haven't figured out that it wasn't me who sabotaged your dreams."

"My dreams were you, Kate. They still are."

Another laugh. Another hollow-sounding laugh. I wanted to grab her and shake her. If only I could make her understand what I was feeling.

To think that I'd once been unable to understand how she'd felt when she was so much younger. What a fool I'd been.

"Your dreams were me." She repeated the words as if she were tasting them, trying to figure them out. "Really? Because you've got a helluva way of showing it. Shirlee Conlee texted me this morning. She's a damn good businesswoman. Far better than me."

She stopped and shook her head. Another bitter laugh. And then she continued.

"Eyes and ears everywhere. She told me I needed to be on the lookout. That Ted Palmer was sniffing around the shops again.

"When she first told me, I thought nothing of it beyond the fact that Ted is an unscrupulous asshole and anyone who would work with him simply isn't a decent person. So imagine my surprise when she tells me that Matthew King is working as his lapdog."

Her words were like a physical punch. One that I rightly deserved.

"I had wondered why you suddenly showed up in my shop." She shook her head again, her gaze falling to the floor and in that minute, I saw the awful sheen of tears in her eyes. I needed to hold her. My body ached to take her into my arms. I'd held her through tears so many times when we were younger. Usually, they were tears that were brought on by something asinine her father had said or the neglectfulness of her mother. The tears I still remembered the most were the tears she'd cried that awful last night we were together.

And now here she was again, crying over me. I ached to reach out and bring her to me, but I was afraid that any attempt to do so would send her flying from the room.

"I'm such an idiot." The words were barely more than a whisper, but they were like a knife in my chest. I'd brought those words out of her.

"You're not an idiot, Kate. You've never been an idiot a day in your life." My hand was still extended toward her, clenching as I attempted to move closer to her, but it just seemed too far to breach now.

"Oh shut up, Matthew." She looked up now, wiping a tear from her cheek angrily. "You know damn well I was an idiot. You banked on me being stupid. I let you back into my heart the minute you walked into that shop. And damn you, but you knew I would too. I mean, I wasn't the one who had all those public relationships with women in town after the two of us broke up. I was the one who couldn't move on. You? You moved on pretty damn well."

"That's not fair, Kate." It was. It was fair, but nothing felt fair at that moment.

"Isn't it?" And now she was glaring at me, daring her to prove her wrong.

"I never got over you, Kate. Everything that happened this weekend between us - everything I said - it was real."

"Was it? Like how you fed me that bullshit about how Ted had bought the Richardson estate and was going to raze it? That was a particularly nice lie. Nice touch, taking me to the place we once said we would raise a family in and tell me about how it was about to be pummeled to the ground."

"That part was true, too, Kate."

"No, it wasn't, Matthew, and you damn well knew it. The house is still owned by poor Richard Finke. He's never sold the thing. No one has even made an offer. No one has contacted him about the house in years. Tried to sell me the thing for a song. I told him I had no use for it."

That last sentence was so bitter that it nearly shook me from the reeling, dizzying sensation that was the room trying to close in on me. How could the house still be owned by Finke? How could it be that Ted hadn't bought the damn thing before he came to me? How had I managed to not even call Richard to ensure it was still on the market?

How in the hell had Ted Palmer bamboozled me from the moment he walked into my office?

I knew how. He'd told me today. He knew everything about everyone in this town, which meant he knew how little pressure he would have to apply to get me moving. When it came to Kate, he wouldn't have to lift a finger to make me jump.

He'd lied about the house being purchased by him. He'd lied about believing that I had moved on from Kate and that this would be nothing more than a fishing expedition for me.

I'd often considered the fact that Ted enjoyed causing chaos in Rainbow Valley. This proved it.

"Believe me, Kate." My voice choked on the words. "He told me he bought the house. Told me if I didn't get you to sell the shop, he would raze it. Destroy the dream we'd once had together. You have to believe me."

Even as I said the words, I realized how familiar they sounded.

"Do I?" Kate's voice raised an octave. "I have to believe you? That's rich coming from you. I once stood before you, begging you to believe me? Do you remember that? How does it feel?"

It felt terrible. Like drowning, and there was no one to help pull me out. I was lost, not knowing what to say and reaching for anything. A life preserver to help me withstand the waves that were crashing overhead.

"If it wasn't you who deleted the email, Kate, then who was it?" The words came out as a harsh whisper, and I wanted to pull them back in as soon as they were out of my mouth. It had been a desperate grasp for the shore, but the only thing it had done was pull me deeper into the tide.

A sound, something between a choke and a sob, sprung from Kate and suddenly we were right back where we were ten years ago. And now we were both drowning.

"I shouldn't have to tell you now and I certainly shouldn't have had to tell you then," she managed. "You believed what you wanted without evidence. As it so happens, I've got way more evidence now to declare you guilty for whatever crimes you're maintaining you aren't guilty of."

I panicked as she turned and reached for the knob. She was about to walk out of my life all over again. She couldn't just walk out again. I couldn't withstand it.

"Kate, wait. Please." For a moment, she stopped, her hand braced on the side of the door that marked a threshold between a life with me and a life without me.

"The only reason I agreed to help Ted was to save the house. Because of what that house had once meant to us. The idea of it being razed, it was like it was destroying any possibility of us being together again."

Her mouth opened to say something and I already anticipated what it was she would say. That I'd already done a fine job of destroying any chance of us ever having something again, but she stopped. Because she knew I already knew what was going through her mind.

Still, she wasn't walking out.

"Kate, I'll do anything to prove it to you. To make it up to you. Just give me a chance."

Seconds passed before she looked up at me and smiled. A sad smile and one that felt more like a nail in the coffin than the tears she had cried earlier.

"Like you gave me a chance?"

She turned and walked out the door, closing the door behind her and closing the door on the dreams that, only minutes ago, had actually seemed real again.

CHAPTER 10

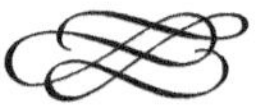

KATE

I cursed the day I'd given Matthew my phone number.

There were many days I cursed when it came to Matthew King. I still remembered the first day I'd noticed him at school. I was a sophomore, and he was a senior. Back then, he was tall and slim. He had that lean bit of muscle a young boy has when he's athletic and knows the value of his body.

There wasn't a head that didn't turn when Matthew King walked through the hallways of Rainbow Valley High. His dark hair flopped over his eyes in that carefree way of a boy who was still getting used to being in his own skin. He always had an easy smile. Being two years older than me, we rarely spoke, but he would sometimes glance over my way in the hallway as we made our way to class. To this day, I still remembered the first time he'd said "hi" as he passed me in the hall.

Back then, I'd been an awkward 15-year-old girl who didn't fit in with any crowd. I wasn't a bully, and I wasn't the bullied. I was too awkward for sports and too shy for theater. I was a middling student who'd rather read a book than bother with extracurricular activities in which I had limited interest.

Boys, however. I noticed them.

And I noticed Matthew King. Most everyone noticed Matthew

King, but I did especially. I was too embarrassed to write his name in my notebooks, as I'd seen Farrah Mansfield do. We'd never been close friends, but we'd had a shared interest in Matthew King. I'd let her fantasize out loud during study hall about all the ways she might get Matthew's attention. She was lucky enough to live on the same street as Matthew and knew things about him I only dreamt about knowing. Like the fact that he'd raised the money himself to buy a used Mitsubishi 3000GT and spent the summer fixing it up himself. She'd regaled me with tales of watching him through her family's den window. Naturally, he'd done most of the work shirtless. To this day, I still wasn't certain whether that part of the tale was true.

Back then, he was all slim boyish lines, but I was still jealous of Farrah. But not jealous enough to turn down an invitation one night to spend the night at her house so we could spy on the object of our affections together. I still remembered the mutual disappointment both of us felt when we'd watched him step out of the house all dressed up and drive away in his Mitsubishi. Likely, he'd been on his way to pick up a date. A date that was certain to be far more interesting than either of us could dream of being.

We'd learned the following week he was dating a cheerleader by the name of Samantha Burlington. Both of us hated her without question. She was perfect and beautiful, with fully developed breasts and long legs she took every opportunity to show off. And while Farrah and I agreed to both hate her without question, we'd also spent the next few months of their courtship emulating her. Then Farrah decided she no longer found Matthew interesting and instead became interested in a guy by the name of Brad Jacobs. Brad was one year older than her and actually showed her some attention. After that, not only had her interest in Matthew waned, but so had her interest in our admittedly weak friendship.

Matthew dated Samantha for most of the year. Samantha once dared to be nice to me by helping me pick up my books when someone had run into me in the hall and sent them flying.

There was nothing worse than finding out the object of your affection's girlfriend was nice, kind, *and* beautiful. Especially when you felt like none of the above.

I barely remembered a time when Matthew King hadn't occupied a huge part of my mind. And now that I'd given him my phone number, he was determined to stay there.

He tried calling. Tried texting. Over the week that followed, the realization that happily ever after would never be a thing for Matthew and me, he'd done his best to get in touch with me. Finally, as much as it hurt me to do it, I blocked his number and attempted to move on with my life.

"Love is a joke," Everly said as she stepped into the shop carrying a box full of donuts. She sat the box on the counter as I scanned through the online orders and fixed me with a stare. I'd tried not to be mopey, but I suspected Everly saw right through that. Everly liked emotions. She wasn't made for pretending that things didn't hurt when they obviously did. She was the type of person who was passionate to a fault.

"I don't know how to fix the stupidity that goes with love, so here's my offering. Donuts from the best donut shop in town."

Turning from the computer, I flipped the lid on the box and bit into one of the sweet confections. For a moment, the sweetness of the sugar was enough to drown in before it all came crashing back down all over again.

For two weeks, that was how it went. I pretended I was okay with everything. Everly would bring in sweets. We would eat the sweets. Day after day, that's what happened.

After two weeks, a customer inquired about the L. Frank Baum books.

And I threw out a price.

I heard Everly gasp behind me. As I wrote up an invoice for the books, she hovered behind me as if she wanted to take the pen out of my hand and force me to put the books back where they belonged. Everly's eyes scanned the invoice, memorizing every detail about the couple's name. Her concern lessened the sting of finally selling the books.

If nothing else, I had a friend who cared. It was a far cry from Farrah Mansfield and our weak friendship based on mutual lust.

"Why did you sell them?" she asked after the couple walked out with the books. I swallowed the lump in my throat and looked back to Everly.

"It's time to move on." The words stuck in my throat, but I worked them out. "I can't do that if I keep hanging on to little things that remind me of a dream that's never going to come true."

It hurt like hell to watch the couple walk out of the shop, but in the end, I knew the only way I'd ever move on was by severing all ties.

Which wasn't easy to do when Matthew moved from his attempted calls to visiting the store in an attempt to talk to me. Each time, I fled to the office like the coward I was and let Everly deal with him. After his third attempt, Everly made her way to my office and plunked herself down in the seat opposite mine.

"What happened?" she asked. It had been the question she'd been dying to ask and after a couple of weeks, she'd finally decided the time had come.

"I let him break my heart a second time. There won't be a third."

I hadn't talked to anyone other than Everly about what happened between Matthew and me. There was no sense in trying to discuss it with my mother or Cassie. They were determined to make every minute of their lives, as well as mine, about Cassie's wedding.

It had been three weeks since I'd seen Matthew. I'd convinced myself that I would be fine with the inevitable dress fitting for the wedding. Cassie wasted little time in picking out both a dress for herself and bridesmaid dresses. Now, I was facing the first of what would probably be many sessions of being measured and prodded for my bridesmaid dress.

It was my sheer luck Cassie had chosen a dress shop close to Matthew's office. The office where he'd broken my heart for the last time.

Lauren Andrews, the owner of a Thousand Times Dress, was wrapping my waist with a vinyl measuring tape. She seemed unaware of how much effort it was taking to not stare out the window.

At least his car didn't seem to be in the lot. Hopefully, there would be no repeats of those days Farrah and I had watched him speed off toward a date with another woman.

"Not a fan of weddings?" Lauren asked, breaking into my thoughts. She was on her knees before me, running the tape from my hips to the floor.

"I used to be." I gave in and stole a glance out the window at the building across the street. Nothing had changed in the last two minutes. Shocker. "Used to think I'd have my own big wedding some-day. Doesn't seem to be in the cards, though."

"It could be," Lauren said, walking toward her tablet and making more notations before winding the tape measure back up and facing me. "You're young. Attractive. Business owner. Intelligent. Perhaps someone is waiting in the wings to take you from sad to glad."

"Am I that obvious?"

"I see a lot of sad and glad in my business." Something about the way Lauren said this made me believe that she'd seen more sad than glad. Possibly in her own life. "I've become accustomed to identifying both on sight."

"No wonder you're so good at finding the right dress for your clients."

Lauren sighed. "Perhaps as a business owner who helps people find the right memory they're looking for, you'll understand. I do it because I've never had the chance to do it for myself."

Again, I saw those L. Frank Baum books walking out the door. I wondered if the couple was pregnant or trying to get pregnant. Maybe they were hoping and dreaming like Matthew and I once had.

Matthew never knew about the books. That was my private dream.

"Well," I began, "you're young. Attractive. A business owner. You're intelligent. Perhaps someone will take you from sad to glad soon."

Lauren laughed. "Touche."

She disappeared with the promise to show me some options for underthings. I groaned, wondering what type of Spanx I was going to have to pour myself into.

I turned back to the window and sucked in a breath as I saw Matthew's car pull up before the building. He stepped out and a thousand little memories pricked at my skin like grains of sand. He looked amazing. He was dressed to impress in a tailored suit that fit him in all the right places. Only three weeks ago, I'd seen what he looked like beneath that suit. Try as I might, I couldn't stop wishing I'd had a little more time to get to know his body as it was now. All toned and made to be worshipped.

I watched as he made his way to the other side of the car and opened the door. My stomach sunk as I watched him help an attractive woman out of the car. As she stepped out, his hand slid to the small of her back as he led her toward the Craftsman. She looked back at him and smiled, laughing at something he said in return to her. He opened the door for her and they disappeared inside.

It was easy to imagine all the charming ways he would charm her once they were in his office. I'd never made it back to his office. Only just inside, where we'd once again torn each other's hearts out and tossed them aside. It was easy to imagine him stepping on a remnant piece of my heart as he stepped over the threshold.

Once again, he would move on.

And once again, I was a fool.

When the nausea started, I'd chalked it up to bad choices in diet. It was impossible to forget what had happened between Matthew and me some weeks before. The potential consequences of that night paled compared to the heartbreak I'd felt.

There had been sweets. The donuts and confections that Everly had brought into the shop. The takeout I'd ordered when I'd was too drained to fix anything healthier.

I'd been too busy nursing a broken heart to consider that the nausea was anything other than a case of feeling like crap.

But then the day had come for my period. Another day followed that one and then another. Before long, I was more than a week late and the warning bell that was ringing in my head told me I didn't need a test to tell me everything was about to change.

It was a Monday before I was able make a trip to Cressfield.

Rainbow Valley was too small to consider heading into a pharmacy and picking up a couple of pregnancy tests. Someone always knew someone and that kind of gossip would be around the town before I could pee on the stick. Telling Everly that I wanted to check on a shop in Cressfield, I was thankful that some new ad technique on social media had pulled her in. She paid little attention as I walked out the shop door.

By the time I made it back to my house and was standing over the three peed-on sticks, I already knew I was pregnant. The certainty seemed to have wrapped itself around me from the time I left the shop until I stood in the bathroom waiting for the timer to go off.

When the timer finally rang out, it was like a gunshot sounding through the house. Taking a deep breath, I looked down and confirmed what I'd already known.

I was pregnant.

Pregnant with Matthew's baby.

I placed a hand on my stomach and breathed in deeply. I was going to take care of this baby and love him or her to distraction. Was I angry that none of this had gone the way I'd wanted to?

A little. Matthew would have been beside me if things had gone the way they were supposed to. If I closed my eyes, I could imagine him bringing his arms around me. I could hear his voice telling me how happy he was. How excited he was to meet our baby. He would kiss me. Hold me. Tell me how this was everything he'd ever dreamt of.

Instead, I was alone.

But it didn't mean I was any less excited about what was to come.

Part of my dream with Matthew included kids. So maybe there would only be one kid.

If she was a girl, I'd raise her to be strong, smart and let no one make her feel like she was less than. She'd be independent. She'd never depend on anyone to feel like a valued person. Not even me.

If it was a boy, I'd teach him to be strong, smart and to honor the women in his life. Not lie to get what he wanted.

I desperately wanted to tell someone about the life that was forming inside me. As it was, my body was rolling through a torrent of emotions. Elation at knowing that there was life inside me. Sadness at how the baby's father wouldn't be a part of this process. Excitement as I wondered what he or she would be like. What it would be like to hold them for the first time. Disappointment that Matthew wouldn't be there with me when the baby took their first breaths.

Right now, I didn't want to tell anyone. First, it was too early to tell anyone. Though the possibility of a miscarriage terrified me, I knew having to explain that miscarriage would make the hurt worse.

But I also wasn't sure how or even if I wanted Matthew to know about the pregnancy any time soon. Eventually, he would find out. And I wouldn't attempt to keep my child from his or her father.

But he'd relinquished any right to be a part of the pregnancy when he'd deceived me for the benefit of Ted Palmer. Part of me knew it was petty to hold on to something so precious, keeping it from him to punish him for his deceit.

Still, I'd finally achieved one small victory. One possible, albeit different, route to the dream having my own kids and seeing them grow. Eventually, Matthew would know that dream as well, just not as he'd likely hoped.

Join the club, Matthew.

For now, this would be my secret. And it was a secret I planned to hold on to for as long as I could.

CHAPTER 11

MATTHEW

Why hadn't I called and checked out Ted's story the minute he walked out of my office? Everything I'd ever learned from slinging real estate told me you always followed up. Take nothing for granted. Make sure your ducks are in a row. But the minute he stepped in with the ultimatum - with the devil's bargain with Kate - I'd fell in line like a silly child.

Ted knew my weakness. He'd told me I was Kate's weakness, but the opposite was true. Kate was my weakness. Ted came into the office, waved the possibility of that old dream in front of me and I'd ran and fetched like a trained dog.

Now that I'd had time to think it over, it seemed obvious what Ted's plan had been. Attempt to get me to do his bidding with the least possible effort on his part. And I'd fallen right into his hands.

While I hadn't doubted what Kate told me about the Richardson Estate, I still had to hear it from the man himself. It surprised Richard Finke he was getting inquiries about the place. For years, it had been his albatross. Now, there were two callers in less than a week.

Luckily, the man was too pragmatic to think it anything beyond a fluke and when I'd made him an offer, he'd seized it. He was glad to be rid of the thing and me?

I was determined to convince Kate that the dream could be ours once again.

Which was going to be difficult. I'd called, but the calls went straight to voice mail. I was pretty sure she'd blocked my number. After that, I'd visited the store. Each time, she was out. I suspected she hid in her office, but pushing my way back there was going to do nothing but make her angrier with me.

If I hadn't known better, I would have thought she was completely over me and wanted nothing to do with me. To move on. But I couldn't accept that. I'd been there that night, just as she'd been. She'd been putty in my hands. I remembered what she'd said to me that night.

"Don't leave me again."

Each time I heard that refrain in my mind, my chest went tight with pain.

I needed to persuade Kate to give me another chance, even if I didn't deserve it. No matter how many times I had to walk into that store and have her evade me, I'd do it to let her know I wasn't giving up on us.

At the very least, I was getting to know her assistant, Everly. I recognized that she stood between a rock and a hard place, but something about the woman told me she was a hopeless romantic. If I could get her on my side, I could possibly get to Kate.

It was sinister, but I'd do worse to get Kate back. I'd wooed clients before. This was no different. She liked the little cream cakes from Francesca Stevens' bakery downtown and I'd bring her a box every day, if that's what it took.

"She sold the books," she said one day when Kate definitely wasn't in. Usually, Kate's car sat in front of the shop, a sure clue she was nearby. This time, however, her car was nowhere to be found. And I suspected that if she saw my car, she would speed on by. Still, I was playing the long game.

"The books?" I asked, realizing that I didn't know what Everly was talking about. She was a cute girl. Not necessarily pretty, but attractive. She had the kind of beauty that reminded one of a little sister. It was as if she hadn't quite grown out of that adolescence that was still breathing down your neck in your early twenties. She had dark hair like my own and I wondered if my brother Adam still had a thing for blondes. They would look cute together.

Not that I'd ever convince him to give Everly or anyone else a chance.

"She used to keep these Wizard of OZ books behind the counter." She gestured toward a shelf that graced the wall behind the counter. There were a few shelves staggered on the wall there that featured an array of curated merchandise. It was easy to imagine Kate chewing her lip as she decided what to display on each shelf. But indeed, an empty spot sat on the lowest shelf.

"Customers would come in and notice them, ask about them, and she would always make an excuse not to sell them. She usually told them they were spoken for. That usually kept people from asking about them further. But as long as I've been here, which is a few years now, they've always been here and she's always refused to sell them.

"I figured she was saving them for a future kid of hers, but last week, she sold them. She'd been hanging onto them for years and she sold them. Just like that."

We were talking about nothing more than a sale of a few books that some children's author had written over a hundred years ago. But the words felt like a gut punch.

"I didn't know about the books," I finally managed.

"Well, now you do." The way Everly said this told me she'd held onto this tidbit the last few times I'd been in the store. Wondering when was the right time to work it into everyday conversation between me asking for Kate and bribing her with sweets.

It was a Thursday when Everly told me about the books. I'd missed two family dinners since the fallout with Kate. There'd been calls from my mother and sister, both curious about what kept me away. There would be no missing another family dinner this week.

I didn't want my family to know what was going on. If anyone could detect the truth on my face, it was my family.

Once in their presence, I couldn't keep up with the good-natured ribbing that came with being around them. Usually, I would join in. Adam, my older brother, was always good for some sort of teasing and Sophie was relentless with the jokes and jabs.

But as much as I wanted to revel in the comfort of being with my family, I couldn't. Everly's words from that afternoon still rang in my ears. Kate had kept those books for a child that she'd dreamt of having and, suddenly, she no longer dreamt about having that child.

I'd destroyed a dream of hers. I'd destroyed my dream as well. And the realization caused a hollow ache in my chest. That ache would never go away until Kate was in my arms.

My aloofness was noticed by all members of the King clan, but none so much as Sophie and my mother. Sophie tried to corner me and get me to spill my guts to her, but I'd rebuffed her at every pass.

My mother, however, was not so easily distracted.

"What's going on, Matthew?" She'd cornered me in the den while the others were outside. Something told me they'd orchestrated the encounter behind my back. Get Matthew alone and find out what's wrong with him.

"You disappeared for two weeks," she continued when I shrugged off her question. "You barely answer calls or texts and then when you finally show up for dinner, you're as silent as the grave. Now, you'll either tell me what's going on or I'm going to start prying."

My mother had always been a hands-on parent. All her kids were privy to her prying, cajoling, and interfering with every aspect of their lives. Annoying, but we knew it was because she loved us. When our father died, she only became worse. Always convinced that something sinister was going to happen to us that would take her children away from her, just as it had taken her husband away.

It wasn't the threat of her prying that got me talking. There was only so much she could find out and, when she did, it would likely be less than what I'd have told her. My relenting was because I didn't feel like making her worry any longer.

So I told her everything about Kate. Everything proper for consumption between mother and son, at least.

What happened between us that night at the house? That belonged to Kate and me.

"I've never stopped loving her. I've tried. God knows I've tried. At times, I even thought I was making headway, but there was nothing I could do to get her out of my mind. I should have gone to her years ago and forgiven her."

"Forgiven her," my mother repeated, her words flat.

I couldn't believe she'd forgotten what led to the parting of Kate and me, but it had been a while. And it hadn't been her who'd lost the love of her life.

"For what she did with my school application," I explained when she remained silent. It sounded so ridiculous now. It sounded like exactly the type of thing that would part two kids, but not the sort of thing that would keep them away from each other for years to come. Not when they loved each other, as Kate and I had. "I get it now. I understood it when she pulled away from me in my office. God, if she felt like that when she was younger, no wonder she'd deleted that email. I might not agree with what she did, but was it worth throwing it all away? I should have done more to assure her I would never leave her."

The thought was ridiculous then. Now, having her back in my arms for one night only, it was even more ridiculous. I wasn't even sure how I had made it ten years without her in my life and damned if I wasn't determined to change that.

"Matthew."

I turned to face my mother. Her hands twisted in her lap. She somehow looked older, with her mouth drawn down and a crease furrowing her brow. No doubt, she wanted to tell me what a fool I'd been to let the school application come between Kate and me. She was likely swallowing her criticism of what I'd done with Ted.

"What is it?" I couldn't stand to watch her struggle with whatever she wanted to say. Tell me I was a fool. I would heartily agree with her.

"I promised her I wouldn't tell you." The words were barely above a whisper, but they felt like a shout. I didn't know what she was talking about. That didn't stop the chill that crept up my spine. I was waiting for the boogeyman to jump out of the closet. The look on Mom's face had gone from tight to downright worried. Scared, even.

"You promised who you would never tell me what?" Whatever it was, I knew it couldn't be good. She stared across the room, her eyes avoiding mine.

"I would have told you years ago, but when she came to me and begged me not to tell you, she was so broken." She shook her head as if she was shaking off something that had haunted her for years. She took another deep breath before continuing. "I should have seen how broken she was. Should have never agreed to this promise. But now I'm breaking it."

"Mom." My voice came out choked. "You need to tell me what you're talking about. Who you're talking about. Are you talking about Kate?"

I had to ask the question. Even if the answer was right in front of me.

"Kate didn't sabotage your school application, Matthew." Closing her eyes, she spoke again. "It was me."

I didn't even realize I was on my feet until I was standing over my mother, looking down at her. She looked so small and tired. The last time I'd seen her look so exhausted and lost was right after my father died.

"It was stupid and I've lived with it for years." She finally looked back up at me and I couldn't look down at her like that any longer. It did something to my insides. I didn't want to see my mother looking so damned unlike herself. Falling back into the chair, I turned from her. I wasn't sure if I wanted to hear anymore.

"She didn't know I'd done it," she continued as I stared ahead at the wall before me. Mom still lived in the same house she'd shared with my father. A two-story suburban home with a wood-paneled den near the back of the house. The room had once been party to kids rough-housing, playing video games, and screeching for our mother when one of us felt wronged by the other. "I know she was scared. Scared of losing you. Scared of losing that dream you two had for so long. She thought she was in danger of losing the man she loved. The man she'd had plans to make a family with.

"Back then, she loved you so damn much. It used to worry me. Worry me she'd somehow convince you to run away with her and I'd never see you again.

"Ridiculous, but after your father." She trailed off and, for a moment, I wondered if she'd let the words hang, saying no more. I almost wished she would.

"I saw how much you loved her." From the periphery of my vision, I saw her turn to face me again, but I couldn't bring myself to look at her. Not yet. "I was certain - absolutely certain - it would all work out.

"She begged me to never tell you I did it. She didn't want me and you to have a falling out like you did with her. She told me she understood why I'd done it. That she couldn't even completely fault me for doing it because she understood my fears, but she didn't want a rift between us. She'd lived with an aloof mother and she wouldn't take away what you had with me."

"Not her decision to make." The words sounded weak, though.

Mom ignored me. "Furthermore, and this is the real reason I never told you, she told me that if you really loved her, you'd come back to her. It would work out in the end. I was so certain that was the way it would happen."

Bracing my elbows on my knees, I bent over, covering my face with my hands. I pressed the heels of my hands into my eyes, trying to push back against the onslaught of memories from that night. I could see her as clearly now, as if it had happened only moments ago. Her face, tear-stained and pained, begging me to believe her.

And I didn't. I'd been so sure.

"Oh, Kate." I hadn't meant to say the words out loud. They'd come freely as if I were trying to conjure her out of thin air. To bring her to me so I could tell her all the ways I'd messed up. "I threw her away over nothing."

"We were all idiots." My mother's voice broke through the hell-storm that raged through my mind. Pulling my hands away from my face, I turned to her. "I should have told you a long time ago. Perhaps I was the biggest idiot out of the bunch, but I always believed you would get back together."

"And now what, Mom? She thinks—"

"Matthew, she doesn't think." Her words cut me off before I could finish the thought. That she thought I'd tossed her aside over nothing. "She knows. You didn't forgive her. And you need to come to grips with what you did to her and fix it. Just like I'm going to have to come to grips with what I did to you. It's a long time coming, Matthew, but I'm sorry. And I hope that one day, you can forgive me just as I hope that one day, Kate can forgive you too."

CHAPTER 12

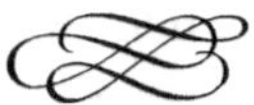

KATE

It had been weeks since Matthew tried to contact me. Despite blocking him on my phone, I was aware of each time he stepped into the shop. Either I avoided him, or I was out on a scouting trip and missed him. In the latter's case, Everly always gave me an update on what he had said and one when he came into the shop. No matter how many times I'd explained she didn't have to, she did it anyway.

And sadly, I wanted to know every morsel, no matter how I pretended it didn't affect me. I suspected that Everly, student of the human condition that she was, also realized how much I clung to every word of her reports.

But then, one day, he didn't show up. And then the next. And the one after that.

Matthew King had finally given up on Kate Cavanaugh. And even though I told myself that's what I wanted, it hurt. It hurt more knowing his child was growing inside me, but it was also a balm. Even when Matthew was gone from my life in the way I wanted him, I'd still have the baby.

I'd told no one about the pregnancy. While I was only a little over two months along, I could feel the anxiety encroaching at every moment. What would my mother and sister say? What would Matthew say? While I had no plans to include him in the pregnancy, eventually he would find out. Eventually, he would be a part of my life again, even if only as a co-parent. I kept remembering how he asked me if I was alright with him making love to me without protection. He had to realize it was a possibility. But was he ready for the reality?

At times, I considered getting in my car, driving out to his office, and telling him. But when he'd eventually stopped trying to contact me, I'd taken it as a sign that it was better to wait to tell him. What if he had already moved on? What if he didn't want a baby?

In the end, I'd delayed the inevitable for as long as possible. No one other than my doctor and Lauren Andrews needed to know until I was showing.

It felt a little easier to step into A Thousand Times Dress today. Matthew's car wasn't parked at his building across the street. Hopefully, I wouldn't see him escorting any attractive female clients inside.

I'd arranged to have the fitting for my dress done privately. After calling and talking to Lauren, I'd found a kindred. Lauren probably heard more stories as a wedding dressmaker than the wedding planner.

"When are you due?" she asked as she invited me into her office. It was early in the morning before her shop opened. Lauren must have heard desperation in my voice. She invited me to come in before the shop opened before I could dissolve into tears on the phone.

"February." I cringed. My sister's wedding was in January. Cassie would be livid when she discovered her maid of honor would be eight months pregnant at her wedding. In any normal circumstance, I would have told her about the pregnancy. My dress would need some adjustments. Big deal, right?

My sister, however, would have howled to the entire town about the injustice. Matthew would find out about the pregnancy within the hour. I knew the easiest thing to do would be to just tell Matthew, but I was a coward. Nightmare scenarios swirled in my mind of what he might say when he found out.

"We'll design your gown with an empire waist. Something that can expand as you grow," Lauren said, looking toward my abdomen and then back up to meet my eyes. "But you need to tell your sister soon. I'm not saying she won't be difficult…"

Lauren had already seen the difficult side of my sister. I recognized the look of someone who had become familiar with the antics of Cassie Cavanaugh. She'd been spoiled her entire life. She wasn't used to being told no. This made for interesting situations when she encountered someone who did.

"Eventually, Cassie is going to find out. I understand why you're hesitant, but it will be better if she finds out from you rather than from someone else. God forbid someone sees a baby bump and tells her."

Luckily, I wasn't showing yet. The changes in my body had been slight. Only a bit of nausea here and there and a slight tightening of my jeans.

As I made my way home after my visit with Lauren, I imagined all the ways the inevitable conversation with Matthew would go. Part of me believed that though he'd be shocked, he would also be elated. And then he would tear down the walls to be involved with the pregnancy.

But another part of me still reeled from what he had done. Maybe he would be angry. This little voice loved to remind me he had stopped calling and coming by. He had given up on me. After all, if he truly wanted me, as he had insisted, wouldn't he have continued to put up a fight?

A tiny voice in the back of my mind reminded me it wasn't fair to expect him to keep trying. Not when I'd made it clear I wanted him gone. He'd respected my wishes and boundaries.

The bottom line was Matthew King was going to be a father. But he would no longer be the man in my life. And somehow, I would learn to be okay with that.

BY THE TIME Everly and I closed up shop for the day, I could tell she was bristling with the need to say something. I'd been distracted all day, trying to pretend everything was fine, but secretly stewing over the fact there were showdowns on the horizon. Not only the eventual confrontation with Matthew but also with my sister and mother.

"You know me well enough to know I'm going to badger you until you tell me what's going on with you. But earlier, I watched some insufferable jackass incorrectly identify a Pyrex pattern, and you did absolutely nothing to correct him."

I bit back a smile. I didn't expect people to know about every piece in an antique shop. But when someone was being insufferable, I usually just had to correct them.

And that guy had been completely insufferable.

But instead of challenging him, I'd let it go.

"Maybe I'm just tired." It wasn't completely a lie. I suspected as the months flew by, it would be more difficult to keep my eyes open longer. Everly wouldn't understand that yet, so I couldn't exactly tell her the reason for my fatigue.

Just like I couldn't tell her the reason I was aloof was because I was constantly thinking about being pregnant.

"How long has it been since you've been out?" she asked.

I shuffled through my mental Rolodex of memories, trying to think of the last time I'd been anywhere that wasn't a dress fitting or a scouting run for the store. The last time I'd been somewhere completely frivilous was the night with Matthew.

And we all know how that ended.

"Awhile," I finally answered.

"Well, that answers that. We're going out and you're going to tell me what's going on."

'Out' for Everly was a little dive just south of downtown. Rainbow Valley could never claim to be big. So, when you told someone a location was just south of downtown, no doubt they had visions of an hour commute to some place in a burb-like setting. But in Rainbow Valley, south of downtown meant you took Main Street about four miles out, drove through three red lights, and bam. South of downtown.

The Psychedelic Mushroom was a little pizza parlor that was more popular with teenagers and those who were attending Ina Palmer, the one college in town. I suspected that Everly had chosen it because there was little chance that we would run into anyone we knew very well.

Anyone like Matthew.

"So, when are you going to tell me?" Everly asked after a large, deep-dish pizza sat before us. It smelled heavenly, and I was thankful the misnamed morning sickness hadn't taken away my ability to love and eat pizza yet.

"Tell you what?" I took a huge bite of the slice I'd picked up and let the warm cheese melt over my tongue.

Everly looked around as if she were in the middle of some thriller instead of sitting in a small town eating pizza with me. Then she leaned across the table and whispered, "That you're pregnant, Kate."

If she had been using a tactic to get me to reveal my pregnancy, it worked. I stopped chewing and stared at the woman before me. She would have made a brilliant detective.

But I knew if she was asking, it was because she knew. Everly was the person who could figure out what was about to happen in a movie before everyone else.

"How did you know?" There was no point in denying it. Once Everly figured out something, bullshitting her was a waste of time.

"First thing, you always tell me when you're on your period."

"I do?"

"Every time. You're never in my face about it, but you always apologize. Because of the cramps."

That part was true. I always took off one day for my cramps, which were usually debilitating. Such a simple tell, but one that would have been immediately obvious to someone as observant as Everly.

"Second thing, we've had a few customers with babies or who were pregnant and, when you didn't think anyone was looking, you watched them. Not in a creepy way. More in a kind of wistful way. At first, I thought it was just, you know, your biological clock ticking."

At this, Everly sighed, and it didn't take a student of the human condition to know she sometimes understood that wistful longing herself. Everly had grown up an only child and though she made little noise about it, sometimes she'd let it slip that she'd also been a lonely child. She wanted a family. She wanted to feel like she was part of a big house full of babies and kids. Kids who didn't have to entertain themselves because there was no one else around for them to play with.

"But it was the way you looked at them," she continued, alternating her sentences by blowing on the hot slice she was holding. "It was wistful, but it also looked like someone expecting something."

Without even thinking, I put my slice down. My hand slid to my stomach. There was nothing there yet, but I knew. And now, apparently, so did Everly. Everly followed the motion with her eyes, waiting for me to say something more.

"The only person I've told is Lauren Andrews and only her because she's going to have to fix my bridesmaid dress to accommodate me, looking like a tugboat."

"When will you tell Matthew?"

I knew Everly and Matthew had become better acquainted over the past few weeks. I was even a little jealous she was interacting with him when I wasn't. Which was ridiculous because I'd cut him off.

"And please don't tell me you're not telling him. That's too stupid for you."

"Of course I'm going to tell him." My voice wavered a little, though. Wavered in the way that told Everly that if it wasn't for the fact he would find out anyway, I'd keep this baby a secret all to myself. "But I'm afraid. He hasn't been into the shop for a while."

Everly sighed. "Yeah. I've missed the sweet treats. It also doesn't make sense."

"Of course it does." I shrugged. "I didn't expect him to keep trying to get in touch with me for years."

"It was only a few weeks."

I swallowed. Everly cringed.

"I don't mean to say he doesn't care enough about you to only give it a couple of weeks before he gave up entirely."

"You didn't have to. And I don't blame you for thinking it because it's what I've been thinking too. It's what I wanted."

"Is it?"

"Under the circumstances, it's what I wanted. He used me, Everly. He used me and, in the process, got me pregnant.

"I knew what I was getting into. At least somewhat. I knew there was a slim chance after our night together I could be pregnant, but what I hadn't anticipated was that he was using me the whole time."

I halted my next sentence when the door to the pizza parlor opened and a familiar face walked through. Everly placed her slice down on her plate and turned to see who had just walked through the door.

"Isn't that Matthew's brother?" Something about the way she asked the question made me pull my gaze back to her.

"Adam. He owns Royal Apple Farms on the outskirts of town."

And just like his brother, Adam was the apple of many a female eye in Rainbow Valley. Unlike Matthew, Adam was quieter and not as quick to pile on the charm. But he was also the guy who helped little old ladies across the street and remembered to ask after ailing family members by name.

He also had one of those tragic backstories that made women dream of being the woman who could "fix him." Adam was older than Matthew. He had found his happily ever after and followed it, marrying his college sweetheart as soon as they were out of school. They'd had it all planned out. The wedding. The house. And soon, the baby on the way. Then she'd died in childbirth. The child too. It had been at least seven years ago, but I still grieved for him.

And now, he was looking our way. Giving us a nod and excusing himself from the hostess, he made his way over.

Everly turned back toward me, fixing me with a stare that was one part anticipation and one part worry. "Are you okay with him coming over here?" she mouthed.

I gave her a look that told her in so many words to keep her cool. Then, I looked up as Adam hovered over the table.

Working on a farm had given him the type of body that put actors who played superheroes to shame.

"It's been a while." He slid a glance over to Everly that made her cheeks pink. That was interesting, but not at all unexpected. Everyone seemed to have that reaction to Adam. The only reason I seemed to be immune was because I was so head over heels for Matthew.

After a brief exchange of pleasantries, I asked after the only other sibling I felt comfortable asking about. "How's Sophie?"

At that, he genuinely smiled, a radiant thing that likely made women's toes curl. "Don't tell me you haven't seen her online. And I mean all of her."

I smiled in return. Indeed, it was impossible to live in Rainbow Valley and not be familiar with the infamous Sophie King. Sophie had a penchant for taking some of the geekiest, yet sexiest photos online.

Turning to explain Sophie to Everly, I realized how ridiculous that would be given that she knew more about social media than I did.

"Adam, this is my friend Everly Lassiter. She's my right hand at Old Things New and one helluva social media maven herself."

And I'll be damned, but Everly blushed. In my time knowing her, I'd never seen Everly flustered. It seemed the human condition had finally bested her as well.

Hmm.

"Do you have a social media presence for Royal Apple, Adam? If not, I'm sure that Everly could help you out."

I was absolutely not going to look at Everly, who I was certain was giving me a death glare. Instead, I turned back to Adam, who had pulled his attention from Everly and fixed me with a quizzical stare.

"No. Social media is for people who have nothing better to do with their lives. It's a great way to piss people off, lose friends, and nosy in other people's affairs. I do just fine with word of mouth and tradi-tional advertising. Sophie uses it, but damned if I have an interest."

I opened my mouth to say something that would smooth over any ruffled feathers, but I didn't know what that would be. I was Kate Cavanaugh, not Everly Lassiter.

Though it didn't seem Everly was any better at figuring out what to say, either. She remained mute.

Finally, she looked up at Adam, fixed him with a glare, and said, "Well, if that's your word of mouth, I'm shocked that you have a business at all, Mr. King."

At that, she made a quick excuse that she needed to go to the bathroom and pushed past Adam, leaving me to figure out what the hell had just happened.

"That wasn't well done of me, was it?" Adam said, watching Everly walk away as he ran a hand through his hair. He turned back to me.

"I could tell you it was all just a misunderstanding, but…"

"I'm sorry. I'll apologize to her."

I shook my head with a sad smile. "I think, when it comes to the King boys, apparently Everly and I are just not that lucky. No offense, but you guys are fantastic at mucking things up."

At that, Adam fixed me with his own sad smile. "You're missed at the family dinners."

"Give your mother my love, Adam."

CHAPTER 13

MATTHEW

*R*arely had I been so fraught with immobility. For weeks after Mom's revelation, I stagnated. Nothing had suffered in my work life. I showed clients property. Brokered deals. Was charming to a fault. I was going through the motions. Nothing more.

But at night, when I was alone with my thoughts, there was one thought that rose above all others.

I had destroyed the love of my life over nothing.

That night, she had begged me to believe her. She'd been terrified I would go off to school and everything would fall apart. All of our dreams, right there to be shattered. And she'd done nothing. She'd let me have my dream, no matter how much she thought it may have destroyed her. She'd leaned right into that adage of letting something go that you love.

And what had I done? I'd broken her heart. If I'd become an architect of anything at that moment, it was the architect of her shattered heart.

I didn't deserve her.

She'd been willing to take the fall for something she hadn't done so I could have something she'd always wanted: a good relationship with my mother.

Mom had given me my space over the ensuing weeks that followed her confession. She'd texted some, and I'd answered her, but I hadn't been back to a family dinner since that night.

While I was annoyed with Mom, the person I was really angry with was myself. Kate had depended on me to realize the truth, to give her the benefit of the doubt, and my pride had won out over my love for her.

It made me sick to think about.

What she was thinking about now. I'd not tried to talk to her anymore since before Mom's confession. Not because I wanted her any less or what we'd had together, but because I didn't know what I was going to say when I finally talked to her. I couldn't talk to her without acknowledging that I knew.

Knew that I'd been the one to destroy everything.

I'd finally convinced myself it would be better to drink the problem away as I sat in my living room staring at a blank TV screen. As houses go, mine had not been what I'd envisioned living in for the rest of my life. It wasn't the "forever home" my clients sometimes joked about when they were looking for the perfect house. It was new construction on the north side of town.

Far away from where I'd once dreamt of Kate and I settling down.

From the house where months ago, I'd made love to Kate for the last time.

No. I refused to believe it was the last time.

I'd been about to pour myself another drink when the doorbell sounded throughout the house. It was a hollow, sterile sound. No doubt Kate would have hated it.

As I opened the door and looked down at my sister, I realized it was Friday. I hadn't even remembered the family dinner this week.

"Sophie." As greetings went, it wasn't the most welcoming, but she didn't need coddling. She pushed her way into the house past me, looking around.

"It's dark and there's no one here." She turned back around to face me.

"Were you expecting a party?"

"To be honest, I don't know what I was expecting. You've been MIA for weeks now. The only reason I know you're alive is this town is worse about gossip than Hollywood."

Sighing and knowing there was no way out of this confrontation with Sophie, I gestured for her to follow me to the living room. I watched her look over the room. Her eyes landed on the decanter, its stopper discarded to the side.

"You've been drinking."

"One drink. I would ask if you want one, but I know you're not likely to be staying more than a few minutes."

"Is that your way of getting rid of me?" she asked. If she thought it was, she was making no strides toward the door. Instead, she flopped back onto my sofa and looked around. "Has anyone ever told you this place doesn't really suit you?"

Yes, I wanted to say. I told myself that frequently, but I remained quiet.

"Why did you buy the Richardson Estate?" she asked.

And there it was.

"For a town that's as gossipy as Hollywood, as you claim, it appears it took plenty of time for that particular tidbit to make its way back to you."

"I've known for a while. I didn't really care until you started disappearing from Thursday night dinners."

"Did Mom put you up to this?" It was a ridiculous question. Mom had little control over Sophie, and it had been that way since she'd been a toddler. Sophie rolled her eyes.

"Have you met me?"

"Fair enough," I conceded.

"So, why did you buy it?"

For a moment, I considered lying to her. Telling her it had just been a spur-of-the-moment thing, or that I had plans to renovate and sell it. It wouldn't be the first flip I'd executed, although I'd largely gotten out of the habit of doing the renovations myself. However, I was tired of trying to hide how I was feeling.

"Because I was in love."

"Was?"

Looking up at Sophie, I picked my glass off the table and downed the rest of the drink. I knew how pathetic I must have looked, sitting in the dark and drinking like some pathetic, sad-sack bachelor, but then, wasn't that what I was?

"Because I am in love." I'd been in love with Kate since I was nineteen years old. It still amazed me she'd been right under my nose for years before I'd noticed her after we graduated. She used to laugh and tell me she'd had a crush on me for years before. I still wondered if she was teasing me about that.

How could I not have noticed her? Impossible.

"You're talking about Kate," Sophie smiled wistfully. I'd never thought of Sophie as a romantic. She liked geeky stuff. Video games. Movies where people clubbed each over the head with swords and the occasional baseball bat. Not even when she was a teenager could I remember her ever delving into romance novels or sparkly vampires. She'd once begged me to take her to a horror movie she wanted to see when she was thirteen. I'd flinched at some of the gore. She'd never batted an eye.

But as I watched her, looking at me a little sadly, I wondered if something was changing about my sister. Maybe there was more hidden there beneath superheroine costumes and video game badges.

"Do you even remember when Kate and I were together?"

Sophie barked out a laugh. "I was 12, not 2. You guys were connected at the hip. And besides, she was nice. Way more girly than me. She liked all the sweet shit. Romantic comedies and stuff. Old Victorian novels with some broody asshole who could never get over his girl."

She stopped at that.

"Guess some things never change."

I raised my empty glass to her in salute.

"But she was kind. Always remembered the things I was into. I got the feeling she knew I felt different from everyone else, and she didn't make me feel weird about it. She was very...mothering."

Yeah. That was my Kate.

My Kate.

"So wait. You bought the Richardson estate because you were in love. Are in love. So where is she?"

"I broke her heart. Twice." My voice sounded choked. Strange. I needed another drink.

"Then unbreak it," Sophie said as if this were the easiest thing in the world. As if she were only telling me how to negotiate a U-turn and not unfuck the last ten years of my life.

I reminded myself Sophie hadn't been in a serious relationship before. Being that strange girl Kate had coddled all those years ago, I wondered if there wasn't something more to it than just comic books and video games.

"It's not that simple."

She sighed. "I'm the last person who should give relationship advice, seeing as how I've never had one."

"And why is that?" I asked before I could stop myself. She was my little sister, after all. If anyone had the right to ask those sorts of questions, it was me.

She shrugged as if it didn't matter to her, but there was something about her demeanor. It was the way I remembered her shrugging off the fact no one had asked her to prom. She'd told Adam and me that it hadn't mattered. That prom wasn't her thing. But I knew better. She'd wanted someone to ask her. For one night, she wanted to be that girly girl, but no one had ever given her the chance to be that girl. Adam and I had played video games with her that night, even though we were both ass at it and she kicked our asses continually.

"Perhaps I'm just hideous."

I snorted. She was my sister, but she was a gorgeous girl and she had a string of admirers online who followed her every move. Honestly, seeing some of the outfits she posed in was enough for me to swear off the internet forever.

"Like hell. You've got a literal fan club."

"Those guys just want the girl who's spent the last hour doing her make-up, pushing up her boobs, and putting on crazy outfits. Trust me, they don't want the real Sophie King. That girl is more comfortable in jeans and a sweatshirt. She sometimes doesn't even brush her hair for two days when she's not doing a shoot. If they saw that girl, they'd block me on every social media channel."

There was no doubt in my mind that she believed that, but I suspected she was the only one.

"And besides, you can't distract me. We're not talking about my love life or lack thereof. You don't just buy a house because you're in love and then mope around for weeks and not talk to the object of your affection. I may not have the relationship experience you do, but I've read enough Superman and Lois Lane to know that's not how you treat the woman you love."

"And what would Superman do?"

"He'd fly over there and get his woman." She seemed to ponder this. "Actually, that's probably not true. He's much more of a broody asshole than people realize. He'd probably do what you're doing and brood and be woe is me for a little while. But eventually, he'd go get her. Marry her and make superbabies."

There was no missing Sophie's wistful sigh.

"Anyway, I'm your little sister. You're supposed to lead by example. I've got two older brothers now who are so miserable they make me want to skip town. You guys are supposed to be a good influence on me. Give me advice, not the other way around."

"Did you stop by Royal Apple and give Adam advice before you came here?"

"No. He was broody last night at dinner. He was rude to some woman at the Psychedelic Mushroom a couple of weeks back and he's still sore about it."

I rolled my eyes. "Can't have him project anything but the mild-mannered man of tragedy, I suppose."

"As if you have any room to talk, brother."

"Touche."

"Get your shit together, Matthew. This is a bad look for you. It's going to give you bad skin."

"One of these days, I'm going to pay you back for all this advice you're giving me and you're going to hate it."

"I'm counting on it."

As I watched Sophie drive off, I pondered Superman and Lois Lane. What little I knew came from a few movies I'd seen over the years, but the part about him flying over and making superbabies with Lois was sticking in my head.

I might not be Clark Kent - that was much more Adam's gig than mine - but apparently we'd both been blessed with finding that one true love.

My dream with Kate had always been to get married and have a family together. No matter my successes in business, there'd never been anything like loving Kate and being loved by her in return. There was only one conclusion to a love that strong: see it to its inevitable conclusion.

How many nights had I dreamed of Kate in a wedding gown? What our kids would look like? Christmases together. Birthdays. Our kids' graduations.

That house was sitting over there waiting for us to fill it with memories, but first, I had to tell Kate that I knew. If I had to grovel for years, I'd make this right. No matter what it took, Kate Cavanaugh would be mine once again.

CHAPTER 14

KATE

I knew the inevitable confrontation was coming. Each day, I grew more nauseated with anxiety. Hurtling toward the second trimester, I didn't think I could blame the nausea on the pregnancy any longer. It was a simple - or in this case, not so simple - case of nerves.

When I imagined telling him, the only outcome I could envision was him wanting to be involved with every step of the pregnancy. After all, this had once been our dream. When I went down this mental rabbit hole, I couldn't stop the onslaught of images that came with it. How different things would have been if it hadn't gone so sideways. There would be cuddle sessions on the sofa with his hand on my belly, feeling the baby move for the first time. Him standing in the doctor's office with me as I found out the sex of our baby.

Now, I was having lunch alone with a midwife my OBGYN had recommended. She'd insisted we meet for lunch when I'd become so flustered over the phone.

Piper Jameson was tall whereas I was short. She had an hourglass figure that reminded me of Jessica Rabbit. Her flame-red hair completed the look. Heads turned as she stood to greet me. When my doctor had given me Piper's name, I'd imagined a matronly woman who would coo me through my labor. I hadn't expected a woman who would make me question my sexuality.

"How far along are you?" she asked once we'd gone through the pleasantries.

"Almost 16 weeks." It had been four months since Matthew and I had made this baby. It seemed like I was speeding through this pregnancy and I'd only seen glimpses of my baby's father. What time I hadn't spent worrying about Matthew and the pregnancy, I'd devoted either to work or Cassie's constant grabs for attention.

"It's getting to the point I can no longer hide it," I continued as she poured some sort of artificial sweetener into a glass of iced tea. "I haven't told Matthew. I haven't told my sister or mother. The former is going to be surprised. The latter is going to be pissed."

"You have no plans for Matthew to be involved in the pregnancy?" There was no judgment in her question. Likely, she knew Matthew in some capacity since the town was so small. A jealous part of me wondered how well she knew him. I pushed the thought aside, seeing how ridiculous the thought was.

"No." I took a deep breath and then followed it up with a gulp of water, my throat dry. "It will just complicate things. I'd rather do this on my own. No more surprises."

Since the day in Matthew's office, I'd heard no more from Shirlee about Ted Palmer or his plans. For a few weeks after, I'd expected Ted to come barging into the shop and demand my acquiescence to his plans. Nothing of the sort had happened, though. It had been quiet on that front.

"What you're most comfortable with is important," Piper said, watching me. "My role is to make this as easy on you as possible. If for some reason you change your mind about anything, I'm flexible."

I could hear the suspicion in her voice. The suspicion that I might change my mind about Matthew being involved. Certainly, when I told him I was pregnant, he was going to do his best to be as involved as possible. The thought already exhausted me. How much easier would it be to let the chips fall where they may and let him come in and take over?

But I'd given him his second chance, and he'd blown it. Now my concern was for my unborn child. Our unborn child. Surely he couldn't fault me for that.

I'd nearly made it back to the shop before I realized that I'd negotiated the drive back on a weird sort of meditative autopilot. I'd followed all the rules of the road, obeyed all the stop signs, and stopped at all the red lights. But my mind had been somewhere else. For the rest of my lunch with Piper, we'd go over things such as birthing plans and things I should do in the meantime. She'd mentioned the Rainbow Valley Birth Center and how I should visit it soon. A comfortable place to give birth and close enough to the hospital to be moved quickly if something went wrong.

If something went wrong.

The other pitfall of being pregnant on one's own was that you had no one to discuss your fears with.

And as if I'd conjured the one that I wished I could talk to about all of it out of thin air, I pulled in front of the shop to see Matthew's car. As soon as he saw me pull up, he was out of the car. And damned if he didn't look as good or better than he had that night we'd made the baby. Dressed in another tailored suit, he leaned against his car as he waited for me to put the car in park and make my way out.

My stomach flipped at how damned good he looked.

What was he doing here now? Had he somehow found out? I was wearing a loose, flouncy top, one that would disguise any hint of a baby bump. Still, I worried he would know the minute I stepped out of the car.

Taking a deep breath, I opened the door and stepped out. I nearly rested my hand on my abdomen, something I'd been doing increasingly over the past few weeks. I'd had to school myself not to do it around my mother or sister, but the urge to let it go there now was almost overwhelming.

"Good, I've caught you." He smiled as he said the words. He had caught me. In ways he didn't even realize. And if I didn't watch my step, he would catch me all over again. And again, my heart would break in two just like it had before. Only this time, I'd be carrying his baby while he broke my heart.

"You're not so clever," I said, putting one foot in front of the other and crossing the parking lot toward him. I left a good ten paces between us. It seemed a safe bet. The shops in the row were all but deserted. It was after lunch on a Monday, one of our slowest days of the week. "I was actually about to come to you."

"You were?" There was genuine surprise in his voice. There was also a hint of hopefulness. It would be so easy to lean into that. I had to keep reminding myself that this was the man who had made love to me, knowing he was deceiving me to help Ted Palmer. The man who had once tossed me aside when he refused to believe me. If I kept all that in my head, keeping him out of my heart would be so much easier.

I motioned for him to follow me into the shop. Everly was standing behind the counter. She took one look at the man following behind me and arched an eyebrow. There was so much said with that one arch.

Are you okay? Do you need me? Should I call the cops?

Years of working together and being friends had afforded me a level of communication with her I didn't have with anyone else.

She must have read my expression with the same sort of fluency. She grabbed her tablet and high-tailed it toward the office.

Without thinking, I moved behind the counter. It was like a fortress that separated me from Matthew and whatever potency his magic might have on me. I placed my purse behind the counter and turned to see him watching me. I clenched my fingers as my hand nearly went to my abdomen. Was something giving me away?

"I bought the Richardson Estate," he said without preamble.

I wasn't sure what I had expected him to say, but it hadn't been that.

"Why on earth did you do that?"

"Because I'm not giving up on us, Kate."

Breathe deeply, Kate. There's a whole counter between you and him.

"You shouldn't have done that, Matthew." I gripped the counter, trying not to let myself give in to the overwhelming urge to run out of the room. I felt a little dizzy. Don't let me faint.

The thought of Matthew catching me was enough to settle me.

"There is no us. I would say that you ensured that by what you did a few months back, but you ensured there would be no us when you tossed me aside eight years ago."

"I never tossed you aside, Kate."

"You did! You didn't believe me. I begged you, Matthew. Pleaded with you to believe that I did nothing you accused me of. Instead, you thought the worst of me. So, yes. You absolutely tossed me aside."

He looked away for a moment, looking out the plate-glass windows toward the highway outside.

I studied Matthew's profile as he looked out at the world beyond the shop. I wasn't sure if it was a personal bias or reality, but he really was one of the most handsome men I'd ever seen. That included all those made-over movie stars and fashion models. He'd always been handsome, even when he was younger and less defined. Now, time had chiseled him into the type of man women wanted to adorn with lingering kisses. I'd felt every plane of his body, and even now, with all my doubts, I still wanted more.

A muscle twitched in his jaw before he turned to face me once again. "I know you weren't the one who did it."

I'd thought him telling me he had bought the Richardson Estate would be the least likely thing I'd expected from him, but this topped it.

"Mom told me everything."

That woozy, dizzy feeling was coming back. I'll be damned if I was going to swoon in my shop. I stepped from behind the counter and made my way over to an antique Queen Anne and sat down. Matthew stepped toward me, crouching down before me. I pushed myself back into the chair, putting as much distance between the two of us as possible. He saw the gesture and sighed, moving away slightly, but still not returning to his full height.

"I asked her to never tell you that. She promised."

Memories of that week flooded my mind. A headache was forming above my left eye. I pressed my fingers to it as if it might push back whatever was causing the pain.

"She saw how unhappy I was after our parting this last time. I guess she figured it was time the truth was known."

Damn her. She had no business doing that.

It was true I didn't want Matthew to lose what he'd had with his mother. But I also wanted him to come back to me because he knew I would never do that. Not because someone had acquitted me for him.

"So that's why you're here." The words were almost a whisper. "You now know I didn't do it, so you think you can finally be with me? Is that it?"

"No!" Matthew gripped the arm of the chair. I looked down at his hand and back up at him. My gaze must have been murderous because he pulled his hand away. "Nothing that happened that night was anything I didn't want to happen. I should have been upfront with you from the beginning."

He dared to pull closer to me once again. The only way to move away from him was to stand from the chair and move away, but at the moment, I didn't feel steady enough to do that.

"God, I never meant to hurt you, Kate. I wanted that house because of what it represented to the two of us. A life for the two of us.

"I never got over you. You mentioned there were others, but they never lasted because they weren't you. I have never stopped being in love with you, Kate. Not for one day. I was an idiot. At first, it was my pride that kept me away from you, and then it was my fear. But at no point did I stop loving you."

"You should have fought for me."

"I should have, and now I am."

"It's too late." Finally, I stood and pushed past him. He was too close and despite feeling out of sorts, I knew I would never feel one hundred percent until I could step away from him. As close as he was, I could smell that clean, masculine scent I used to drown in. I walked to the office door, gripping the handle. I knew that Everly was on the other side, no doubt hearing everything we were saying. I didn't care.

"It's never too late." He followed me to the door, but kept his distance.

I steeled myself before I looked back at him. It was now or never. I turned.

"There's something you need to know." I closed my eyes, feeling like I was about to dive into the deep end of the pool. "And before I tell you, you need to understand it changes nothing about how I feel. There's no way to repair the damage that's been done to us."

What I hadn't said was that there was no way to repair the damage that *he* had done to us.

"Still, you deserve to know."

He was staring at me, confusion marring his features. And me? I was forcing myself not to close my eyes as I took the leap I'd been dreading for weeks.

"I'm pregnant, Matthew."

A host of emotions crossed his face in a few seconds. Shock. Hope. Fear. Want. Possibilities.

"Kate." The way he said my name nearly made my knees buckle. His voice was husky but choked. I had to get out of this situation. He stepped toward me. I twisted the knob behind me. A sure sign that if he came any closer, I would disappear behind the door and not come out again. He stopped.

"You deserved to know." I was proud of myself when my voice didn't crack. It wasn't full strength, but I didn't sound like a whimpering fool, and that was good enough for me. "And when the baby is born, I'll do nothing to get between you and him."

"Him?" His voice cracked a little at that. I cursed myself for the choice of words.

"Or her. I don't know yet." I looked away, unwilling to fall into the trap of looking into those dark eyes and letting them pull me in again. The way they'd pulled me in and led to all this. "The baby deserves a father, and I won't take that away from them. But this doesn't change things between us. And I can handle the pregnancy part of this. I've handled it well so far."

"I should be there." His voice was a little stronger. More forceful. I sighed. I expected no less from him. Still, I shook my head.

"My heart is still broken, Matthew. The baby inside me doesn't change that. It just gives me somewhere else to focus my energy."

"Let me be there for you." He was pleading.

"Now, if you don't mind, I have some work I need to finish because I'd like to get home early."

"Kate…"

I turned the knob behind me.

"Turn the open sign over as you go out, please."

"Kate, let's talk about this…"

"Please, Matthew. Just…please." I closed my eyes, willing this conversation to be over before I lost it. Opening my eyes, I saw him give me a final nod and turn. I watched as he walked out the door and got into his car before driving away.

But I wasn't fool enough to think that Matthew King was giving up so easily.

CHAPTER 15

MATTHEW

*P*regnant.

Kate was pregnant. Pregnant with my child. Our child.

And I couldn't touch her. Couldn't feel the way her body was changing as our child grew in her womb. I thought of the baby moving inside her. How I would miss that. My fists clenched and unclenched as if I could will her to my side, bring her to me, and feel all those subtle changes.

I'd known something was off the moment she stepped out of the car. We'd always had a sixth sense about each other, but it was the blouse she was wearing. Billowy. Almost peasant-looking. In the time I'd known Kate, she'd never chosen that type of look. She'd never been a waif. She'd always leaned into her curves. She liked more conforming clothing. She liked clothing that allowed her to move. No fabric to get in the way. No billowing material that snagged or pulled on something.

It was such a simple thing. And yet it told me something was different.

I never would have imagined that the something different was her being pregnant.

Kate getting pregnant had once been a part of the Big Dream. How many times had I dreamt of her carrying my child? What she would feel like as she grew heavier with the pregnancy?

I wanted to be angry at Kate for denying me access to this part of our child's development, but I had no right. I'd earned her denial and more.

More than anything, I wondered how she'd found out. If she'd been scared. The stress had probably kept her up at night. Wondering how to tell me. When to tell me. If she even would tell me.

I'd broken her heart. That's what she had told me. And I'd spend the rest of my life trying to make up for it.

She just had to let me.

And I knew Kate well enough to know that she knew I wouldn't give up. Somehow, someway, I'd be a part of this pregnancy. I didn't make it as far as I had by being a man who gave up. I'd already decided before I knew about the pregnancy to fight for Kate.

Now I was going to fight for Kate and our baby.

I'd just have to convince Kate to let me be a part of the pregnancy. The question was how.

I didn't want to tax her. I didn't relish the idea of stressing her out, especially with her pregnant.

I'd have to be the best expectant dad in the world. That was the plan. Operation Best Expectant Dad in the World.

The night after I'd found out about Kate's pregnancy, I'd drown myself in Google Fu. I knew when she'd gotten pregnant. That information allowed me to calculate how far along she was with the pregnancy.

According to Google, our child was about the size of an avocado. Apparently, sizing unborn babies by the size of fruit was a common thing, but seemed like a sort of weird marker. Then again, who was I to critique?

Given where she was in the pregnancy, she'd likely gotten over most of the morning sickness. It annoyed me that I'd missed helping her through even that. I could have made her tea. Held her hair when she threw up. All things I'd thought I'd do with Kate when we were younger and the dream was still in place.

I might not have been there for the morning sickness, but I'd be there now. Even if I had to do it from twenty feet away, I would be there.

Not knowing exactly where to start, I went with the old standard. Bribing Everly and potentially giving Kate a little treat as well. Instead of going to Everly's favorite pastry shop, I made a B-Line for Kate's favorite donut shop instead. I'd googled all the best foods for pregnant women and while donuts weren't on the list, I figured she could toss the whole thing into the trash if she felt like it.

I had to start somewhere.

Walking into the shop, I saw a box with legs walking toward me. Everly was on the phone behind the counter to my left. She looked over at me and raised an eyebrow.

The box with legs was Kate.

Throwing the box of donuts onto an antique table near the door, I rushed over toward Kate and hefted the box from her hands. Kate's look of surprise was almost enough to wash away the annoyance that she'd not asked for help with the box.

"Where do you want it?"

Kate huffed. It wasn't heavy. Just cumbersome.

There was a reply on the tip of her tongue that would have suggested a location for the box that wouldn't have been the least bit comfortable for me. I could see the moment she bit back the reply. I would have enjoyed the tête-à-tête, but she seemed unwilling to even give me that much.

After directing me to a spot near the counter, I could hear Everly stifle a laugh. She then continued to go over the intricacies of an order with a phone customer.

"No, sorry. I had something in my throat. Continue," Everly said into the phone as I turned back to Kate.

Kate had her hand on her hip, giving me a look of annoyance. Yet, the only thing I could think of was how beautiful she looked. Ten years of rarely seeing her and then seeing so much of her that it had led to us making a baby had me realize how badly I'd missed her. After we had parted, I saw her everywhere, despite her being nowhere. But now, I'd had another taste of her and was hopelessly addicted again.

I could also see that she was no longer hiding the pregnancy behind billowy tops. The bump was small, but noticeable. My throat grew a little sore as I looked at her, glowing with pregnancy. It took my breath away.

"I know what you're doing, Matthew." She seemed unaware of my sudden emotional distress. Unaware that I'd glimpsed the slightest peek at our unborn child.

"It won't work," she said, still unaware that I was taking in the sight of her. Her words brought me back to the present.

"I brought you donuts," I said, as if that was an appropriate response to her shutting me out. Walking backward toward the table where I'd tossed them, I picked up the box and handed it to her like we were both teenagers again and just as awkward. She hesitated for a minute before taking the box from me. Then, she took the box to the counter and sat it before Everly. Everly, never one for denying a sweet treat, popped open the box and took a bite, never deviating from the conversation she was having over the phone.

"Matthew—"

"Kate, you can't expect me to stay away from you. You know I'd been trying to reestablish contact after that night."

For a moment, her expression changed at the mention of the night we'd shared. I could still hear her telling me not to leave her again. I'd told her I'd never let her go again, and I was determined to deliver on that promise. Just as soon as that troubled expression had appeared, it was gone.

"As I recall, you tried to reestablish contact, as you put it, for about three weeks after that night. And then you disappeared. Again."

There was no disguising the hurt in the word 'again.'

"I disappeared because my mother told me the truth about that night and it threw me. That's not an excuse, but it's what happened. As soon as I got past it, I came to you. I meant what I said that night, Kate. I'm never letting you go. And I'm definitely not going to stop trying to be a part of this."

I gestured toward that gorgeous swell of her stomach. Her hand went to the bump. My hands itched to reach out and cover hers.

"You can try, but..."

The entry bell rang as the front door slammed open. Kate and I turned to see Cassie, standing in the doorway, looking every bit like fury personified. Before I could even parse what was happening, Kate stepped in front of me, facing down the fury before her. Cassie was only a bit taller than Kate, but somehow, Kate seemed to have the more menacing presence between the two of them. I'd always figured it was because she'd had to stand up to her parents, whereas they'd always given Cassie the benefit of the doubt.

"You cannot be pregnant, Kate."

The words hit me like a punch. I stepped up behind Kate until my front brushed her back. For once, she didn't back away. She nearly leaned back into me. I knew she didn't know she was doing it, but I wasn't moving.

As far as Cassie was concerned, I hadn't even spoken. I wasn't even sure if she'd noticed me. She was fuming. Why, I couldn't quite figure out. Was she actually pissed that Kate was pregnant?

"You can't be pregnant. I'm getting married in January. You'll be eight months pregnant when I get married! You'll be a barge! I need my maid of honor to be my wing woman in January. Not getting ready to have a baby."

"This baby will be your niece or nephew, Cassie." I knew the situation was getting to Kate. To a casual observer, she looked stoic, unbothered. But the time that we'd spent away hadn't dulled my knowledge of all her emotional tells. Her breathing was slightly elevated. I could tell by how she'd squared her shoulders, and they shuttered a little on each exhale. It was slight and, knowing how little her sister concerned herself with Kate's feelings, I doubt Cassie realized it.

Worse, I doubt she even cared she was upsetting her pregnant sister.

"I should have known it would be yours," Cassie said, looking over Kate's shoulder at me. Her voice was much too snide for a girl who was so clearly in the throes of soon-to-be wedded bliss. "She was always stupid about you."

If the situation had been different, I might have felt like gloating. As it was, my senses were too aware of Kate's distress.

"I can't do this right now." Kate's words came out as little more than a whisper. That quiet shutter that only I noticed had progressed to something more visible. Something that Cassie no doubt noticed now, but didn't care to acknowledge. There was a slight tremor in her shoulders that told me she was barely holding it all in. At that point, I didn't know if my presence was helping or making things worse, but I couldn't let her face her sister alone.

From behind me, I felt Everly approach from the counter. Looking over at her, I could see that she was as unhappy about the situation unfolding as I was. She was also just as clueless about what to do about it.

Kate, however, wasn't. She turned and pushed past me, hustling toward her office.

"That's right, Kate! Just run away!" Cassie yelled out after her. For the first time since I'd arrived, I noticed a customer standing near the door, pretending to look at some knick-knacks on a shelf. Her eyebrows were raised in a frozen state of interest. Seeing that she didn't seem to be a local, at least I was certain that what had happened here wouldn't enter the local lore anytime soon.

The door to the office slammed behind Kate. I turned to look down at Cassie. I had a good seven inches on her. And I was going to use every inch.

"You're not going to make this pregnancy hell for her, Cassie." My voice was menacing, and she rewarded me for it with a flinch. I didn't have any desire to scare the wits out of the girl, but there was no way in hell I was going to let her run roughshod over Kate. I'd grown weary of her family neglecting her years ago. Now? I wouldn't let them stress out Kate while she was carrying our child. "I won't let you."

"Is this some sort of threat that I'm supposed to take seriously?"

She was playing tough, but she was enough like Kate that I could tell when she was bothered. Her nostrils flared. Her hands twitched.

I took one step forward. Cassie took a larger step back.

"She's pregnant, Cassie. With my child and your niece or nephew. I won't let you stress her out."

"Right." She looked a little smug. "I suppose only you have that luxury."

I had to give her credit. She'd scored a hit. And she knew it. It was enough of a hit that I softened for just a minute.

"You're right. I haven't been the best for her, but that changes today. And it changes with not letting anyone make her uncomfortable about her pregnancy. Including you."

"Oh, screw you." Finally, she turned and stomped out of the shop, the door slamming behind her as the entry bell once again jingled. The customer in the corner had been staring at the same bird figurine for the past fifteen minutes. I was tempted to ask her if I could help her with something other than the local town gossip.

"That went well," I said, turning toward Everly, who was standing behind me. She looked up at me with a sardonic grin.

"She's going to be hell on wheels," Everly said, walking away and making her way back behind the counter. She slid a loving glance toward the box of donuts before she looked back my way. "Which means you better be on your best behavior."

"I have every intention of doing everything in my power to take care of Kate."

"If she lets you."

"She will," I responded confidently. "She needs someone to be there for her during this. I had no intention of letting her go before I found out she was pregnant. And now I'm determined to make this pregnancy as easy on her as possible."

"And what if the best way to make it easy on her is by removing yourself from the situation?" She picked up a donut from the box and tore into it with gusto.

"Do you honestly believe that she'd be better off with no one there to help her out? No one there with her to be with her when she goes into labor?"

"Maybe she's already got a birthing partner." She shrugged as she said this, but I felt ice flood my veins at the thought of it. Had she?

Everly laughed around her bite of donut. "Easy there, cowboy. As far as I know, she hasn't asked anyone to assist with the birth yet. Likely if she did, though, it would be me and not the 6 foot 5 adonis you're no doubt envisioning."

I must have looked like a bull ready to rage in the china shop that was Old Things New. Everly sighed, opened the donut box once again, and pulled out a donut. She wrapped it in a napkin and offered it to me. For a minute, I stared at her outstretched hand as if she'd lost her mind.

"Kate hasn't eaten lunch," she said. I retrieved the donut from her hand. "It's not the best nutrition, but she should eat something."

Nodding to the woman behind the counter, I made my way back to the office and to Kate.

CHAPTER 16

KATE

When I'd told my mother and sister that I was pregnant, I knew they wouldn't be happy for me. After all, why should they? I was unattached, and it was obviously unplanned. I figured the most I could hope for was that they'd be non-judgmental.

My mother hadn't been excited, but she hadn't dissolved into tears or anger, which I figured was a win.

I also gave her the gift of telling Cassie about the pregnancy. This was one part cowardice on my part and another part letting my mother have the upper hand. This was the juiciest piece of gossip she'd likely ever handled. I'd expected an angry text, maybe even the silent treatment for a while.

What I hadn't expected was Cassie barging into the shop, ready to battle.

And I hadn't expected Matthew to be in the room when it happened.

When he'd stepped up behind me as Cassie raged, I'd felt the warm, broad expanse of his chest millimeters from my back. It had taken all my willpower not to lean back into him and let him drag me away from all the turmoil. There was no doubt that he had taken my refusal to step one step away from him as a tiny victory.

The door to the office squeaked, and I looked up, seeing Matthew's head peering in. I swallowed a sigh as my stomach flipped. There probably would never be a time where Matthew's mere nearness wouldn't affect me, no matter how much I wanted to push him away. Keeping my heart safe was going to be a 24/7 ordeal.

"Everly said you haven't eaten today." Pushing the door open a little further, he stepped in, all 6 foot something of him, and brandished a donut before me. The office was small, having barely enough space for a desk and the person behind it. His presence in it almost made me feel like Frodo to his Gandalf as he towered over the desk. I took the donut from him, trying my best to avoid touching his fingers, but failing. The spark that lit as our fingers brushed caused me to jerk the donut back toward me.

Once the donut was in my hand, I sat it before me on the desk, unable to contemplate the idea of the sugary treat. My stomach was still in knots from my altercation with Cassie. While I stared at the donut, Matthew looked around the office. Eventually, he pulled the other chair in the office closer to the desk and situated his long legs between the desk and the chair. He would have appeared comical if he wasn't so good-looking.

"I agree with Everly that it's not the best nutrition for you, but if you've eaten nothing, you need a little something."

"I'll eat it soon enough," I said, my voice sounding petulant. It was only four more months until Cassie's wedding. Topped with a developing pregnancy and trying to juggle my feelings for Matthew, I already felt exhausted.

"I'll go get you something. Anything you want."

"I'm fine right now, Matthew. Really." I leaned my head back against the back of my chair and closed my eyes, willing the world to disappear for a little while. "None of this is going how it should."

The statement left a lot unspoken. How it should have gone, if what we had originally planned was the blueprint, was that Matthew and I wouldn't be involved in this stalemate. We'd be married. He would have found out about the pregnancy at the same time I had. He wouldn't be attempting to weasel his way back into my life after breaking my heart.

For the second time.

I was a raging idiot.

"You don't have to do this alone, Kate." His voice had always made my heart speed up. It was a deep, resonating thing that injected itself into my veins as surely as if he had loaded it into a syringe and shot the sound straight into my heart. "You need someone beside you, to support you. You don't have to do this on your own. There's no reason you should. Especially when you've got that to deal with."

He gestured with his thumb toward the sales floor where my sister had just delivered her foot-stomping fit. I wasn't sure if she had stomped her foot in retrospect, but when I went over the memory in my head, my mind put the stomp in there.

"I've been dealing with *that* on my own for years."

"Kate, I want to be here for this."

This was the sales pitch. Matthew was not just Matthew King. He was also the king of selling people on their dreams and he knew mine better than anyone did. I wanted to clamp my hands over my ears so he couldn't weave his magic spell over me.

"Is this going to be the hard sell or soft? You can sell my dream better to me than you can sell most people."

I was rewarded with a blaze of anger in Matthew's eyes. It was what I wanted. I wanted a fight. I wanted him to rage at me.

But that bit of fire also showed me that I wasn't another sales pitch to him, which defeated the purpose of baiting him. It did me no good to bait him because his ire was quickly tamped down.

"Dammit, Kate. You know you're not a sales pitch. And I know I've been a raging idiot. You know I know that better than anyone, save for you. I spend every night struggling with sleep, wishing for a way to go back and fix everything that I've messed up.

"I get you don't trust me. I would say that you can't be angrier at me than I am at myself, but I'm not quite that self-absorbed.

"But Kate, I want to see our baby grow and that includes before he or she is born. Let me be a part of this. Don't take this away from me."

Dammit.

I gripped the sides of my chair, wanting to blow up at him, but knowing how futile it was because I wanted him to be a part of this, too.

I could do this. I could let him be a part of the pregnancy and not fall in love with him again.

Mostly because I had never fallen out of love with him.

But I could keep him at bay, couldn't I? Just because he was a part of the pregnancy didn't mean we were a couple. We were two people who'd made a baby and we're doing our best to ensure that baby made its way into the world as healthy as possible.

People did that all the time. Why couldn't we?

"I'm going to regret this."

Matthew leaned forward in the chair, eager now that he realized he was about to get his first concession in this little war of ours. He looked so much like the young boy that I'd fallen in love with that I had to fight to suppress a smile. When I managed that, I counted it as a victory. I could do this. I could let Matthew King be a part of this and keep my cool.

I'd consider it practice for all those moments when I would have to parent a kid who was acting ridiculous but needed some tough love.

"We're going to have ground rules."

"Ground rules," Matthew repeated. There was a note of distaste in his voice as he repeated the words, but he knew he was on shifting sands and didn't risk his footing by questioning it.

"And we're going to establish those ground rules now. This is not a relationship. This is you and I dealing with this pregnancy that we've made. You can go to the appointments. You can be there when the baby is born."

I fought the urge to close my eyes at the onslaught of mental imagery that accompanied that last statement. The thought of holding his hand, crying on his shoulder. I'd heard women say that during those last few hours of labor, your dignity left the room. I'd be at the mercy of my emotions in those final hours and God knows what I would do or say. I didn't have to be a seasoned midwife to realize I would give in to the urge to cry on his shoulder or hold on to him when the pain got to be too much.

That would be something we would discuss later. Right now, we'd take baby steps.

"What about classes?" Matthew asked. "I realize that starts a few months later, but I'd like to be there for that as well."

Damn him. He'd been googling all this. One night and he was already an expert. As I studied him, I saw the dark circles under his eyes. I wondered if he'd slept at all. I wouldn't feel sorry for him, however. He was due a few sleepless nights. I'd had plenty myself.

"If you're going to be there for the birth, you'd need to be there for the classes, I suppose."

He looked almost smug in his victory. I couldn't stand it.

"But the first time you get out of line, Matthew—"

"I'll be on my best behavior."

I rolled my eyes like a teenager. He wouldn't stop trying to convince me of his desire to be more that a co-parent.

"And from here on out, I'm taking care of you," Matthew then added.

My foot shot out, kicking the back of the desk that separated my legs from Matthew's. I may have growled. This would be his tactic. Take on the role of the caring minder until I was putty in his hands.

Until the next time he decided he didn't need me or wanted to use me.

"That's *not* part of the agreement, Matthew. I don't need a minder."

"I have no intention of being a minder." There was something about the way he said the sentence that made my stomach drop. It was in the thing he didn't say. He had no intention of being a minder because he wanted to be something very different. "I meant exactly what I said, Kate. I'm going to take care of you. If you have a craving at midnight, I'll be the one who goes and gets what you want. If you need your back rubbed, I'll be the one to do it."

I would not let my breath hitch at the thought of his hands on me. It was ridiculous. Before we'd broken up, we'd been together for two years. His hands had been on every inch of me at one point or another, and here I was, acting as if he'd never touched me.

I currently nestled the evidence of his prior touching in my womb.

"And I'll be the one to deal with your family when they do idiotic things like your sister just did."

I laughed.

"I can promise you that you're not ready to deal with my family."

"Aren't I?" He raised an eyebrow in challenge to me.

A swarm of memories flooded my mind.

The incident occurred on what seemed like any other day to me. My grandmother's health had been failing since I was 16. The burden of her care had fallen on my Mother and me. On the day that had leeched into my memories, I'd been juggling all sorts of things. School. A part-time job. My relationship with Matthew. Not to mention being the dutiful daughter to my mother and father. Cassie had been in her senior year in high school. My parents decided she was too busy to do any of the stuff my mother and I were doing for my grandmother.

I hadn't meant to forget to pick up the prescriptions that afternoon. I had a final the next day and work the day before. Matthew had picked me up from work to take me home and have some downtime before he helped me study for my final.

It should have been a simple act of forgetfulness to remedy. Remind me of my oversight. I would then run to the pharmacy, pick up the prescription and deliver it to my grandmother post haste.

My father hadn't seen it that way. He stomached my mother's dotage on my younger sister, but I was fair game. And so he unleashed his temper on me, citing my inability to remember to get the important stuff done. The dressing-down he'd given me that night had been thorough. I'd become so used to his dressing-downs that I barely blinked when the words and snaps began. He'd never raised a hand toward me, but he didn't need to. I felt the impact of his words as if they were a slap. He'd never forgiven my mother for not having a boy. He knew she wouldn't consider Cassie strong enough to weather his outbursts. He deemed me able to weather the storms.

I was the one who took the brunt of him that day. I knew as much as he did that he wasn't angry about the prescription. He was angry, and I was as good a target as any.

Matthew and I had only been dating for a couple of months at that point. It was a miracle that my father had waited that long to introduce him to his temper toward me. My initial thought wasn't to think that what Matthew was seeing was a gross injustice toward me. It was complete and utter mortification. Because, even though I knew that the prescription wasn't really the impetus for his anger, I still felt like I'd let everyone down. Him. My grandmother. And weirdly enough, I somehow felt like I'd been a disappointment to Matthew at that moment. After all, who wants a girlfriend who can't even be bothered to pick up her grandmother's prescription? Never mind that I'd done it a thousand times and would have done it that day if my mind hadn't messed with me.

If I closed my eyes, I could still see Matthew standing up from the sofa. He was all long legs and young man, at that strange place between what he was now and what he'd been before. As my father railed at me for those first few minutes, I snuck glances at him. I watched his face go from astonishment to rage. Until finally, he'd stood up to his full height.

He might have been over 20 years my father's junior, but he towered over him. My father was a proud man, but even he couldn't resist taking one step back.

"With all due respect, sir," Matthew began, spitting out the word 'sir' with an impressive amount of vehemence, "there is no way I'm going to stand here and allow you to talk to her like this."

He didn't raise his voice. It was cool, controlled, but menacing. I'd no doubt of Matthew's masculinity, but that was the moment I realized just how capable he was of defending his turf.

And protecting what he considered as his.

My father fumbled in the face of Matthew's fury. He'd tried to at first come back. But when he saw the rage in Matthew's eyes, he backed off. He was also embarrassed to have someone witness one of his rage fests. It was simply the first time someone had met his rage with theirs.

After his confrontation with my father, Matthew had squired me away in his beat-up Toyota. I cried as he maneuvered the car with one hand while massaging my neck with the other.

As I looked at the man across from me, I noticed all the differences and similarities between the young man he was then and the dashing man he was now. Instead of the Henley and jeans he'd been wearing that day, he was now wearing a tailored suit. His shoes no doubt cost as much as half of my wardrobe combined. The beat-up Toyota was gone and replaced with an expensive luxury car that would likely not be fit for driving an infant around town.

But that same protective, attentive man was still there. Just grown with a bit more crinkles around the eyes than he'd had back then. I'd been a fool to think I could keep him at arm's length during this pregnancy. And I'd be a fool to think I wouldn't have to work twice as hard to protect my heart from the man who'd never given it back to me.

CHAPTER 17

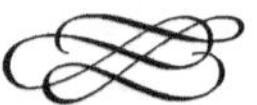

MATTHEW

I'd formed an informal partnership with my unborn child. A sort of in utero Parent Trap.

Stick with me, kid, and I'll see that you have the biggest Big Wheels on the block.

Yes, I wanted to be a part of the pregnancy, but I also wanted to be Kate's partner. I'd messed up my first and second chances, but now I would fix all that. I'll be damned if I wasn't going to grab the bull by the horns. I had always intended to make Kate mine. It had been my fault I'd gone about it the wrong way, but I was going to convince her she was mine.

Because she was. That had never changed.

Weeks had passed since I'd discovered that she was pregnant. Each week, it became a little more difficult for her to hide the progression of the pregnancy. There was no doubt the life inside her was growing. She couldn't feel the baby moving yet, but it was only a matter of time.

And, of course, Kate was still apprehensive about me. I didn't blame her. I'd screwed up royally, but that hadn't stopped me from doing what I had to in order to be kept in the loop. If my unborn child was an accomplice in Operation Win Back Kate Cavanaugh, then

Everly Lassiter was the Q of our operation. Everly was giving me the benefit of the doubt. She was stealthy, and beneath her ballsy demeanor, she had a strong romantic streak. She kept me abreast on when Kate hadn't had lunch, if she was hinting toward a certain craving or any other number of things that she thought I should know.

She was also highly protective of Kate. I knew she would destroy me if I even considered stepping out of line.

When we'd formed our alliance months ago, I'd envisioned her telling me when Kate was having a bad day and I needed to keep my distance.

What I hadn't envisioned was the call that came that afternoon.

"Something bad's wrong," Everly said as soon as I answered the call. Three words and my body was frozen. My heart flip-flopped. Despite the warm weather, I was chilled to the bone. Those three words could mean anything.

Instead of asking questions, I grabbed my keys and left the office.

I needed to get to Kate.

"I'm heading out the door now, Everly." My voice sounded far away. Even with all the strange emotions running through my body, the words came out flat. "Is an ambulance on the way? Should I go straight to the hospital?

I was amazed that I was able ask questions when tiny explosions were going off in my head. I slid into the car and gripped the steering wheel. Other questions pummeled me. Was she in pain? Was she scared? Were we losing the baby? Images of her in pain and scared flashed through my mind. I hastily pushed them all away lest they threaten my ability to get to her in one piece.

"She's not at the hospital. She's outside in the car and she can't get in. They're surrounding the car."

Everly sounded almost panicked. She typically had a cool demeanor that rarely wavered. In place of a visible emotion that might give her away, she delivered a cutting remark or joke. This Everly was scared and that terrified me.

"I've already called the cops, and they said they're on their way, but I knew I needed to call you."

I took a deep breath. "You're not making any sense, Everly." I swallowed curses and demands, determined not to lose my cool with the woman who was my lifeline now.

"They're protestors." Her voice went from a near panic to a strange calm as she launched into an explanation. "I still don't understand what they're protesting, but she's in the car and they're surrounding it. They're also at the door of the shop. Some of the other shopkeepers are trying to pull them away from the car - from Kate - but one shopkeeper has already been punched."

If Everly's first attempt at explanation had failed to make me understand what was going on, her second had only further confused me. I threw the phone down onto the console and sped toward the shop. There were days I cursed the smallness of Rainbow Valley, but today, I was glad for it. It took only eight minutes to make my way to Old Things New. As I approached the little row of shops, I saw a patrol car pulling into the small parking lot that was nestled against the shops.

Kate's car sat before the row of shops, surrounded by people shouting and holding signs. In the middle of the fray, Kate sat in the car, looking lost and confused.

I was out of the car at the same time as the deputy. I recognized him from high school. He had more hair back then, but I recognized his face. Paul Lambert had become a well-known fixture on the Rainbow Valley Police Force. Supposedly, he was the new "Officer Friendly" who went to the elementary school and taught kids how to deal with everything from what to do when a stranger approaches them to how to respond if the house is on fire.

"Stay back, Matthew," he called out as I made my way toward the crowd of people who were shouting and pushing up against the car.

"Kate's in that car and she's pregnant!" I shouted as if he wasn't already heading toward the fray.

"And you'll do nothing but put her in more danger if you don't let us handle it."

Another officer had already stepped in, trying to pull people away from the car. The protestors were shouting any number of slogans, none of which seemed to mesh with the other protestors around them. And absolutely none of what they were shouting made any sense.

As soon as I saw an opening, I rushed toward the car, throwing open the car door and pulling Kate into my arms. I carried her into the shop, her body shaking within my protective hold. There was no pretense as she clung to me tightly, burying her face in the crook of my neck. As I cooed to her and pushed through the throng of people, I met Everly's worried gaze as she pulled us into the shop and slammed the door behind us, locking it. Settling Kate into a nearby antique chair, I hadn't even noticed that Everly had disappeared, only to reappear with a bottle of water, thrusting it into my hand.

I crouched before the terrified woman before me. I'd seen Kate upset before. I'd seen her angry, sad, confused, and defeated. But I'd never seen her terrified. Not like this, and it made me want to go outside and destroy everyone in the parking lot who'd put her in this position.

My hands ran over her body as she shook. I looked for anything out of place. Cuts, nicks, bumps. Anything that might have happened between the time everything had seemed normal and everything had gone sideways. My hands came to a stop at the swell of her abdomen. I ran my hand over the bump, sucking in a breath. I made sure she was okay, but also reveled in the feelings of a father who was, in a strange sort of way, touching his child for the first time.

Kate was too far gone to notice my perusal of her body. I pulled my hands away from her, twisting the cap from the water bottle. She grasped at it as I brought it to her lips.

"Small sips. Don't gulp." Normally, Kate would have balked at my demanding tone, but she only held the bottle, her hands shaking. I cursed at the sight of her, so upset and shaken. For what could have been minutes or hours, we went through a routine of little gestures until I calmed her down enough that I didn't worry about her health or that of the baby's. She would take a sip. I would run my hand over her hair, murmuring soothing words and assuring her everything would be alright, even if I wasn't sure of that myself. I'd ask if we needed to go to the ER and Kate would shake her head and say she was fine, just shaken.

We did this repeatedly until the Kate I knew slowly emerged from the shaken shell that she had retreated into.

Outside, as Everly and I stood vigil over the shaken Kate, the protestors slowly dispersed. Everly handled Paul when he knocked. He inquired about Kate, wanting to know if we needed any further help. Before long, the protestors were nothing more than a memory. Other than a few of the neighboring shopkeepers stopping in to check on Kate, the maelstrom of activity came to a complete halt. Once Kate was calm, I looked to Everly.

"Tell me what in the hell just happened here." I was crouched before Kate. My right foot was going to sleep, and I adjusted my stance. It made the most sense to stand and bring some circulation back to my extremities, but I wanted to be as close to Kate as she would allow me. My hand was on her knee now. I had no intention of removing it until I absolutely had to.

"It made absolutely no sense," Everly began, rubbing her hand over her face. She had been scared, worried for Kate, and she was just finally coming down from that fear. I owed her more than just sweet treats. She'd been genuinely worried about her friend. She looked exhausted. Both women needed the rest of the day off. I'd cross that bridge when we came to it.

"They came out of nowhere. None of their messages seemed to align. One was saying something about how the shops were bad for the economy - as if that made any sense. Another was shouting about rent hikes. It was all haphazard. The only thing they seemed in line about was the fact that they all seemed to want to go after Kate the minute she drove into the lot. I was at the counter on the phone with a customer and it all happened so fast..."

She let out a shuddering sigh. My expression softened as I watched her. Her quick thinking had helped keep Kate safe. It was impossible for me to repay her for that.

"Everly, they're gone now."

"If I'd paid attention to what was going on before she drove up, I could have gotten to the car. I could have got her to the shop before it all started."

"And potentially gotten yourself hurt in the process," Kate piped up. Some of the color had come back into her cheeks. Her voice wasn't as strong as it normally was, but I saw the embers of a fury that stemmed from seeing her friend put in such a position. "You did exactly what you should have done by calling the police and then calling Matthew."

She turned, looking from Everly and back at me. There was something undefinable in her expression. But it was gone just as quickly as it had appeared.

Still, the implication was there. She was glad that I'd shown up.

"But why?" Everly asked, breaking Kate and I from the staring contest we were having. "Who are these people? Why are they showing up here now?"

"Ted Palmer," Kate and I said in unison. I closed my eyes against the guilt that came over me. I'd given Ted a chance. Reluctantly, I pulled my hand from Kate's knee and brought myself to a standing position.

Everly looked from me to Kate and back again. I sighed, knowing that after today, she deserved as much of an explanation as anyone.

"A few months ago, when Ted realized I wouldn't be as amenable to his schemes as he hoped, he suggested he could make life difficult for both Kate and myself."

"Somehow, you forgot to mention this to me," Kate accused. She sounded tired, and I realized she thought I had once again failed to be truthful with her.

"By that time, you weren't speaking to me and when you finally were, I had honestly forgotten about it. Ted says a lot of stuff trying to seem like a badass, but typically he's all smoke and mirrors."

I watched as Kate reasoned through this explanation and recognized the moment that she accepted it. Letting out a breath, I continued.

"My theory is that he's trying to make these buildings seem less attractive to the current tenants. Ted's under the impression that if he can get one of you to fold, the others will fall in line."

"But why focus on Kate?" Everly asked.

My mouth opened, beginning to give my theory, but Kate cut me off.

"Because I'm the weakest link," she said. I began to protest, but she continued. "I've always known that I make the least amount of money of the shopkeepers here. Pushing antiques isn't as lucrative as the other businesses here on the row. While Old Things New is my main and only source of income, Ted also knows that it barely pays the bills. He's hoping he can keep firing until I surrender. He knows that the shop is a passion project, not just a means of paying the bills. He knows that there are better ways to make money, and he hopes he can make me give it up. If he makes it less appealing to me, then I'll sell. And just one vacant shop will make the entire row start to look less appealing to both shopkeepers and customers. He'll do something to the vacant storefront that will piss off all the others. Eventually, he assumes they'll find new digs and he'll get exactly what he wants."

The way she disparaged her dream made me want to throttle Ted. It also made the guilt that threatened to overtake me every night before I went to sleep even more palpable.

Kate ran a hand over her abdomen and I swallowed a curse. Not only because I wanted to do that with such ease, but because I was angry as hell that her pregnancy was being made even more difficult by Ted's machinations.

"Okay, so if Ted is behind all this, can't he be, I don't know, taken to task for it?" Everly's eyes were volleying between Kate and I, wanting answers that neither of us could give her. I knew that with Everly's talents, she could work anywhere in town - or in the country, for that matter - but she stuck by Kate. Everly was the sister that Kate needed. That alone made me feel more brotherly to her.

"Ted would never directly hire these people," I explained. "He probably had someone facilitate the entire scheme in such a way that he would keep his hands completely clean. He's been doing this type of thing for a very long time. He knows how to be underhanded."

"Why on earth did you ever try to bargain with him, Matthew?" Kate asked.

I turned back to Kate. She was wearing her weariness like a cloak. "Because I'm an idiot, Kate. Because I thought he had our future in his hands. He knew how to manipulate me, and he did. I'm not proud of it. The only thing I can say is that it's not just your weakness, he knows, it's mine as well. And my weakness is you."

For a moment, no one said anything. Kate didn't flinch as she watched me and I prided myself on not falling at her feet, though I certainly would if it would help matters.

Beside me, Everly cleared her throat and said something about needing to finish up a phone call from earlier, as well as something about memorizing the "Conjunction Junction" episode of School-house Rocks.

"So what now?" Kate asked once Everly had disappeared into the back of the store.

"I'll deal with Ted." I was relishing the idea of getting my hands on the man. "Right now, you're coming to stay with me, though."

At that, Kate was on her feet.

"Like hell I am." The shaken woman from earlier was gone and in her place now was a raging vixen, ready to do battle. I wanted to pull her to me and crush my lips to hers.

"Kate, I'm trying to keep you and our child safe. While I don't think Ted would deliberately try to hurt you, I question whether or not one of his schemes might go sideways. It almost did today. I'm not taking that risk. Either you come stay with me, I come stay with you, or I sleep on your doorstep. You choose. Because I am damn well going to take care of my family."

CHAPTER 18

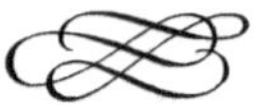

MATTHEW

Kate insisting on my staying at her house instead of mine was an added boon in my favor. The house was small and charming. Perhaps I was reading too much into it, but playing house in such a small space would give me an advantage on the whole pre-parent trap scenario I had going.

If I faltered for a minute in believing I would eventually win Kate back, the whole scenario would have been painful. It was a reminder of what I'd been missing for ten years. Ten years I could have been with Kate. When we were younger, we'd never experienced the intimacy of living together. Both she and I had lived at home with our parents. There wasn't any time to maneuver around each other in the bathroom or get used to one another's nightly routine. I realized now that we had stolen all our moments.

And now I was living with Kate, with our child growing inside her, and I'd never been farther away from her.

Still, within one week of our living together, I'd learned more about her in those days than I had anticipated.

In the mornings, I suspected she had at one time woken up and fixed a pot of coffee. Even though she had likely endured months without a morning cup, she would still walk toward the coffeemaker, stare at it accusingly for a moment, and then walk away with a sigh.

In the evenings, she would wrap up in the frayed afghan on her sofa and channel surf, so studiously ignoring me that I wanted to shake her.

The way she ignored me was so deliberate, I knew it was less annoyance with my presence and more that she was trying to keep her self-imposed distance.

And if I had any doubt of that, other things would demonstrate that Kate was struggling as much as I was with the situation. I'd been in her house for a week and I'd created my own routine that centered around Kate. I reminded her of her prenatal vitamins in the morning. I fixed her dinner - something that was difficult to do when she would attempt to beat me to the punch. My legs were longer, and I was determined. I drove her to work and picked her up from work.

All of this had the very real side effect of placing us close together and driving me insane with the need for her. So, in our own ways, we were both struggling.

The need to pull her to me when she was wrapped up on the sofa was overwhelming. As I slept on the sofa after she'd retired to her room, I dreamt of stomping into her room. I'd peel every inch of fabric from her body and love her until her voice reverberated throughout the little house. And dealing with a stiff cock when she was so close, yet unable to touch her, was torture.

And my body knew every movement she made. At night, I could hear her turn in the bed. At midnight, I would hear a dreamy sigh and my balls would clench, wanting to make her make those sorts of sounds and more while I was inside her.

My dreaming mind made things worse. Some nights, I would be certain I was still awake. I'd walk into her room, find her lying out of the covers, and sink down beside her. My dream would allow me to lavish her body with kisses, coaxing her to the point she begged me to take her. Just as I sank inside of her, I'd wake panting and desperate, so close to giving in to the temptation to go to her.

When we were both awake, I would watch her in those moments

when she wasn't as aware of my presence. She'd gotten more accustomed to resting her hand over the growing swell of her abdomen. As I watched her hand graze over the bump, I wished for the ability to touch her so freely.

"There's not going to be any cuteness," she said to me as we drove toward the obstetrician's office for what would be our first appointment together. I'd done a decent job at covering my nervousness. Today, we would find out the sex of the baby and I would hear his or her heartbeat for the first time. It had seemed real since the moment that Kate had told me she was pregnant, but there was something about the appointment that had my heart hammering. And if Kate's fidgeting in the passenger seat next to me was any indication, she felt the same way.

"No hand-holding," she continued, and I nodded, gravely. "No sentimental bull shit like you see in the movies with the crying and all that."

I knew Kate well enough to know that she was covering her nervousness with ridiculous demands. There was no doubt in my mind that I knew that Kate thought her requirements were ridiculous, but I let her have her coping mechanism. If anything, it gave me something to focus on as my nerves threatened my sanity.

"I can't promise that I won't get emotional," I said as we pulled into the parking lot.

"Fine. But keep it to yourself."

A smile threatened to break through my gruff expression. From the corner of my eye, I could see her giving me a stern look that looked as threatening as a Care Bear. When her expression grew a little more annoyed, I attempted to school my face. Given how impossible it felt not to smile at her attempt to be tough, I felt I did a fairly decent job.

I did my best to keep my distance as the doctor came in, introduced herself, and got down to the business of introducing me to my unborn child. I tried not to stare as Kate's abdomen was exposed and I got my first look at how her body had changed with the pregnancy. As Kate looked toward the monitor, waiting for the sound of a heartbeat or the image of the child inside her, I reached inside the neck of my collar to adjust it. The room seemed hot, the air stale. My hands felt clammy, but I was determined that I wouldn't give in to my nervousness.

I was so focused on my distress at first that it took me a minute to realize that Kate was growing agitated. It wasn't until a second technician stepped in that I realized something wasn't right.

"What's wrong?" Kate asked. I stepped closer, driven by the catch of fear in Kate's throat.

"We're having just a little trouble finding the baby's heartbeat," the technician said with a strained smile. It was the sort of smile that told me that, while this might be a routine glitch, she was preparing herself to deliver bad news if necessary.

Kate turned to me and all bets were off. I didn't worry about if I should or shouldn't. I was next to Kate before I knew what I was doing, taking her hand in mine. Her eyes were glossy with unshed tears.

"It has to be okay." Her voice was barely above a whisper. On the other side of Kate, I could hear the technician trying to soothe her, but the effort was wasted. Instead, I leaned down over Kate and used my other hand to brush her hair from her face.

"It's going to be okay," I lied, cooing to her and swallowing my fears. Why couldn't they hear the heartbeat? What was wrong? I choked back every insecurity and concentrated on Kate, who was steadily losing her battle with staying calm. "I'm right here."

Her hand was gripping mine fiercely. At some point, I wasn't sure what I was saying. I was just trying to keep her from losing her cool. There had to be an explanation. At some point, I heard myself telling Kate that it was just a glitch. Just give it a minute and it would all be fixed.

And I hoped like hell I was right.

I wasn't used to seeing Kate lose her cool. Typically, she handled stress and sketchy situations like a seasoned pro. But it wasn't every day that one was stuck in a car surrounded by a mob or worried that something was wrong with the child inside you. This baby had to be okay. Because I didn't know what it would do to us if everything wasn't perfect.

Suddenly, a rhythmic pulsing filled the room, and Kate's face transformed from one of fear to one of overwhelming relief.

The doctor and technicians were talking. Neither Kate nor I seemed to hear a word any of them said. We were too caught up in our shared relief to worry about it for long. I didn't even realize I was bent toward Kate, placing kisses on her forehead until I pulled back, looking down at the mother of my child. She smiled as she stared back up at me.

I knew even as the moment enveloped us that it would be short-lived, but I simply relished the feel of Kate's hand squeezing my own. At that moment, we'd needed each other. All the weirdness of the past few months was forgotten.

We barely registered anything that was happening in the next few moments. Eventually, I looked at my child's image on the ultrasound screen. Then I heard the doctor say to us, "It's a boy." My mind filled with a strange, cottony feeling. Nothing felt real. The world looked gauzy.

Looking down at Kate, I couldn't resist the urge to bring her hand to my lips, placing a tender kiss on the knuckles. She looked up at me with a curious mixture of joy and worry.

"Everything's going to be fine, Kate." I wasn't sure if I was telling her so much as I was telling myself, but the only thing I could hope was that I was telling the truth.

CHAPTER 19

After the ultrasound debacle, Matthew became even more protective and doting. The urge to let him be that doting and protective partner was nearly overwhelming. Each time I ducked his sweetness, I felt a bit like Wonder Woman. It was a Herculean effort to pretend that I was immune to him. In the weeks that followed the ultrasound, he tried everything to get under my skin.

I suspected he wasn't even trying. He was just being. I'd never doubted Matthew wanted to be a husband and father. It was the fact that I couldn't get over the deception that led to this pregnancy that kept me from falling into his arms.

And they were glorious arms. Not that I had forgotten what he looked like without a shirt. But in a small house with one bathroom, sometimes I would catch a glimpse of him without his shirt. On the night that I had conceived, there'd only been the moonlight to provide light for our interlude. Now, anytime I caught him without a shirt, it was right there before me in high definition. I saw every slope and plane. The definitions of his toned biceps, all olive skin begging to be caressed, within reach. That toned six-pack he had worked so hard for over the years made me want to run my fingers down the ridges of his abdomen.

My pregnancy hormones weren't helping a damn thing, either. Which just made it even more necessary to control my emotions. I didn't know what I was truly feeling. My hormones were making a mess of everything. Day after day, week after week, the reality of the situation became more real. Now that I could feel the life inside me moving, I was going to have to work harder to guard my heart.

Luckily, I had my sister, and mother to keep me tethered to reality. Today was the big cake testing day. While it was more pleasing than fittings or visiting venues, I knew I was going to be subject to comments from the peanut gallery that was my family.

"You're already so big that you're going to look like a whale when it's time for my wedding," Cassie said as soon as I made my way into the backseat of her car, pulling the seatbelt over my middle. I watched her as she watched me, cataloging every eye roll and gesture, certain that there would come a day that I could throw them all back to her.

"I'm 22 weeks pregnant, Cassie. I'm perfectly sized for where I am in my pregnancy." I waited, hoping our mother would pipe in with some anecdote from one of her pregnancies. Instead, she continued to stare at her phone and remained silent. A little backup would have been nice.

"You're small-framed," Cassie said, pulling away from the curb. "It makes you look like a mutant."

"You're even smaller than I am, Cassie." Cassie had always been tiny, taking more after our mother than I did. "Imagine what you will look like when you're pregnant."

Cassie opened her mouth. Then her mouth closed with a click. I smiled at having gotten one in on her. She'd finally realized that eventually, all the jabs would come back to haunt her. I knew it would be short-lived, though.

The bakery Cassie had chosen to create her wedding dream was on the main row of shops in downtown Rainbow Valley. Spoonful Bakery was as well known for its pies, pastries, and baked goodies as it was for its elaborate confections that graced more than half the weddings and events in Rainbow Valley.

As we stepped into the bakery, the sweet scents comforted me like the warm embrace of a lover. I eyed each row of sweets behind the glass cases as we waited for the owner to greet us and take us back for Cassie's tasting.

"Trust me, you don't need anything in here, Kate," Cassie said. Her eyes slid to my middle and, sadly, my hips. "You're going to be big enough in January without any help."

Hearing a stifled gasp from my right, I turned to see a younger woman's eyes volleying between myself and my sister. My sister, who was now busy looking at a display cake with Mom, had completely missed the gasp. The woman and I shared a knowing look before she reached into the case before her. She selected a danish, placed it in a paper wrapper, and handed it to me over the top of the counter.

"Our treat," she whispered as she looked from my sister's back to me again. When I balked, she shook her head and thrust the confection toward me. Smiling, I took the treat from the girl, noting her name - Claire - on her name tag and then biting into the apple-filled danish. The decadent flavors caressed my tongue. I couldn't repress the near orgasmic sound that sprang forth as I tasted all the sweet flavors.

The noise brought Mom and Cassie's attention back to me.

"Really, Kate? You couldn't wait for a few more minutes?" Cassie shook her head. "Pathetic. She'll be a barge by the time the wedding arrives."

As Cassie turned around, I stole a glance at Claire and gave her a sugary smile. Rolling her eyes in my sister's direction, she then gave me a knowing smile before turning to greet a couple who walked in behind us.

The woman behind Spoonful Bakery was Francesca Stephens. I recognized her from her infrequent stops into Old Things New and had even noted that some fixtures in the bakery had been purchased from my shop. After she greeted my sister and mother, she came to me, taking my hands and looking me over.

"Is it forward of me to mention that my associate Claire is Sophie King's best friend?" We were now in the backrooms where several cakes had been set up, ready to be sampled. Beside me, I felt Cassie growing irritated that she wasn't the center of attention.

"Not at all," I said, smiling and wondering what had been said behind closed doors about Matthew and I's "arrangement." "I think pretty much everyone knows that Matthew and I are having a baby. And I'm certain Sophie is going to be a wonderful aunt."

"She's going to want to dress him as a superhero, you realize?"

Beside us, Cassie snorted, and Francesca turned to them, straightening her shoulders. She sent one last telling glance my way and delivered the spiel. There were lemon cakes, white cakes, and chocolate cakes. Cakes with ganache or buttercream. Cakes drizzled in syrups and jams. As she went on about the various pros and cons of this cake versus another, my mind drifted off to what it would have been like to plan a wedding with Matthew. No doubt, he would have wanted a big wedding so his whole family could have come along.

Swallowing a sigh, I envisioned walking down an aisle in a white gown and seeing him waiting for me at the end of it, his eyes shining with love. That was the dream we'd once had. A big wedding, a nice honeymoon, and then a life of making babies together.

Instead, we'd done it all backward. All of our well-laid plans had been torn asunder years ago and had only been stomped on recently. I didn't regret the baby that was moving inside of me as I thought of smashing wedding cake into Matthew's face. Forcefully.

As I bit into a slice of lemon cake, I closed my eyes, letting the sweet and tart taste push the thoughts of my non-existent wedding out of my mind.

"I must admit, that's my favorite, too," Francesca said, as I opened my eyes to see her watching me with a sly grin.

"I was partial to that myself," my mother said, eyeing me as I placed my fork back onto the plate. Ever since I'd told her about the pregnancy, she'd seemed quiet about the whole thing. Part of me thought it might be the fear of becoming a grandmother. The other part of me suspected she wasn't happy with the way I'd gone about making her into one. While my family had always seemed okay with Matthew as my romantic partner, there was still a part of them that didn't like the idea of me as a single mom. Now? One of their daughters would be a perpetual single mother. Despite all the strides to make single motherhood accepted, my family still prided itself on its backward values.

"We're not doing lemon." The words were forceful and surprising, even coming from my sister. She looked to Mom and then back to me as if she was formulating some sort of conspiracy between the two of us. "Honestly, who even considers a lemon cake for a winter wedding?"

Looking over at Francesca, she gave me a smile that told me she didn't take the slight as a personal insult. Whatever my opinion was on the matter, Cassie was going to have the opposite opinion.

As Mom and Cassie debated each option, I took a seat in the corner of the room and focused on the fluttering inside me. The baby had only started moving in my 19th week, but since then, he had been growing more animated. Given how apt he was to move around, I thought he would be more like Matthew than me. Matthew was always moving, always up and about. The other night as I watched him driving the car back from work, his fingers drumming the wheel, I felt the baby move inside me. The baby seemed to move around almost in rhythm with his movements. I'd nearly told Matthew that I thought the baby was going to take after him. Then swallowed the thought, continuing our awkward stalemate.

In moments like this, when it was so obvious that there was an emotional gulf between myself and my family, I wondered if I could give in to the desire to be closer to Matthew. What would it hurt to let him hold me at night? To touch him? To experience that same passion that had led to this situation?

But almost as quickly as my brain began to play with such a scenario, I was reminded of the two greatest hurts of my life. When Matthew had refused to believe me when we were younger and when I'd discovered he had been in cahoots with Ted Palmer. I'd even begun to rationalize the latter. It wasn't hard to believe that he had reacted rashly when Ted had told him he'd bought the Richardson Estate. That he had bought it right after he'd found out the truth about Ted's lies told me that, on some level, he'd been truthful that day.

In the end, I felt it was more that I was afraid. Though what I was afraid of at that point, I was no longer sure.

I'd spent so long going over the possibilities for Matthew and me in my head that I hadn't realized that Cassie had come to a decision. Something with white chocolate. I tried not to make a face. Cassie knew I hated white chocolate and I couldn't help but wonder if that had influenced her decision. Still, it was her wedding. And she was still due a bridal shower.

Which I would have catered with a lemon cake and white chocolate.

Francesca and I shared goodbyes with her, promising that she was going to come in soon to buy some tables to replace a few in the eatery that needed replacing. When she asked if the baby was moving, I invited her to feel for herself if she felt comfortable. When Claire cooed at the idea, I invited her over as well, feeling a bit of a kinship with her after our shared treat. While I wasn't keen on strangers placing their hands on my abdomen, I liked the two women in Spoon-ful. They seemed like kindreds.

Once the cooing was over and I was out the door, I saw that Mom and Cassie were already in the car and waiting to leave. Given the look of annoyance on Cassie's face, I steeled myself for whatever was coming and slid into the backseat.

"Honestly, Kate, do you have to make everything about you?"

Taking a deep breath, I did the one thing I knew I shouldn't do. I took the bait.

"What exactly did I do, Cassie?"

"Well, first, you somehow divert the conversation to your baby and Matthew from the minute we begin," Cassie said, one hand on the steering wheel and the other gesturing in the air. "Then, you do that stupid display where you invite everyone to feel your belly like you're some sort of fertility goddess."

I snorted. "First, I didn't invite everyone to feel my belly. Francesca asked if the baby was moving. The baby is moving, so I told her she could feel for herself. I know Francesca as a customer of Old Things New. When Cassie all but asked if she could, how could I say no?"

Truth was, I hadn't wanted to say no. I liked Claire. She'd been kind to me, which was more than I could say for my sister or even my mother at this point.

"If you're jealous that you haven't been able to feel your nephew move, you're more than welcome to feel for yourself."

"No, thank you." She might as well have been telling me to throw myself out of the car given the venom in her voice. "Just in the future, when we're doing things pertaining to my wedding, don't make your mistake the center of attention."

My blood ran cold. In my lifetime, I couldn't remember wanting to throttle my sister. I'd made jokes about it. But that actual urge to hit her had never been one I could say that I'd felt.

But right now, I wanted to slap her.

Her eyes met mine in the rearview mirror, and I could see the moment she registered the rage on my face. To her credit, she looked almost shocked at what she saw in the reflection.

"My baby might be unplanned, but don't you ever say to me he was a mistake."

Turning to my mother, I fixed her profile with a gaze. She hadn't turned around, but her jaw tightened. I clenched my fist as I looked at her.

"What about you, Mom? Do you also think your grandchild is a mistake?"

For a moment, no one said anything. I could see Cassie's hands gripping the wheel tightly, betraying the cool exterior that she was hoping to convey. Mom's fingers were pulling at her well-tailored dress slacks.

"Well?" I prompted when no one spoke.

"You have to admit, Kate, your timing could have been better."

"My timing could have been better," I repeated, letting the words settle over my tongue like the sugary flavors I'd sampled earlier. The flavor bouquet of these words was acidic and tart, though. If any flavor were perfect for the two other women in the car with me, it was a harsh, unkind flavor. Like sand and vinegar.

When the car rolled to a stop in front of my house, I didn't waste any time. Gathering my handbag, I clicked the seatbelt off. It looked as if my mother wanted to say something to stop me, but I didn't wait for something I knew wouldn't happen.

Instead, I marched into my house. I didn't look back at the car pulling away. Instead, I did my best to quiet the warring emotions that were taking over my body. After I'd grabbed a water, sat down, and calmed myself, I grabbed my handbag and made my way to my car.

There was someone I needed to talk to and the conversation couldn't wait until later.

CHAPTER 20

MATTHEW

When I'd first bought the Richardson Estate, I wasn't sure what to do with it. The plan, when Kate and I had originally dreamed of owning the house, was to treat it like an ongoing project that we'd renovate over the years. Kate always had an eye for what looked great. That was something that bled over into her ownership of Old Things New. She would choose most of the furnishings and decide on things such as paint colors. I'd be the brawn. I'd envisioned myself standing on a ladder, moving paintings from the left to the right until I got it exactly how she wanted it.

After buying it, I'd been immobilized not only by Kate's refusal to see me but then later by my mother's confession. Still, when I had time, I did what I could to bring the house up to code. Here and there, I added furniture with the mental caveat that Kate could do away with anything she wanted to. I simply had the idea that maybe, perhaps, we could bring our baby home to that house. We could at least get that part of the dream right.

Kate, of course, hadn't budged on her refusal to see us as anything other than two people involved in a joint project that ended with us raising a child together.

She'd done everything possible to put distance between us. She was determined to ask for as little help as possible. So, I'd done my best to anticipate her needs. I brought her lunch. Kept an ongoing dialogue with Everly that allowed me to know when she was having a rough day or if something was going on that I needed to be aware of later.

It was a bit like rubbing my stomach and patting my head at the same time.

And God, how I wanted her. Wanted to touch her. Hold her. The closest I'd gotten was the few times she'd invited me to feel the baby move. What no one had told me was that feeling your child move inside the love of your life's body was one hell of an aphrodisiac.

Worse yet was that I knew, on some level, she wanted me too. But she was determined to deny it. I hid just how much the whole thing was driving me crazy. I'd earned her fury and if I spent the next twenty years paying for it, well, so be it.

As I sat in my office, pondering how I could get Kate to meet me halfway in this venture, the woman herself stormed into my office. I jumped to my feet as soon as she breezed in, looking like fury and beauty all at once. Kate was always beautiful, but there was something about her when she was angry that made her look almost goddess-like. There was a hint of color on her cheeks and her pupils were large. It wasn't unlike Kate when she was aroused. Tamping down the thought, I crossed the room, shutting the door behind her and leading her to the chair opposite my desk.

"What's wrong?" I asked as I took the seat on the other side of hers. If things were different, I would have taken her into my arms, placed a kiss on the top of her head, and led her to tell me everything that was going on.

"Do you think this baby is a mistake?" she asked, placing a hand on the top of the bump. Of all the things I had expected her to say, that wasn't on the list at all. I felt a strange sort of fury building inside me.

"What? Kate, God, no! You can't possibly think that. Who on earth told you I thought our baby was a mistake?" Whoever it was, I would destroy them. I couldn't imagine who would say this to Kate, but whoever this faceless person was, I wanted to kill them.

"No one told me you thought it," she said and fell back against the back of the chair. She looked tired and weary. My arms ached to pull her to me, to try to ease some of the stress that she was under. "I went to the cake tasting with my Mom and sister."

I couldn't hide the sound that accompanied the swift intake of air. Her mom and sister weren't bad people, but I'd grown accustomed to the way they either neglected or underestimated Kate. I knew Kate loved them and that they were the family of a child that was to be half mine. Still, someone should have knocked their heads together years ago for the way they treated Kate. Couldn't they see how amazing she was? Was it that they did and they couldn't deal with it? I suspected that might be the partial truth on the part of her sister.

"Your mother told you that this baby was a mistake." I'd tried to modulate my voice, but it sounded clipped and angry even to me. Surely this woman couldn't say such an unkind and horrible thing about her own grandchild. I watched as Kate's nostrils flared at the sound of my voice, much too low and dangerous for me to be talking about my unborn child.

"My sister was the one who said it." She shook her head and I could see the weight of those words pulling down on her. She'd been angry when she'd come into the office, but as she sat before me, some of that anger had deflated. I wanted to revel in the fact that she had come to me for comfort. Not Everly. Me.

"But my mother didn't correct her," Kate continued. "Just said that my timing could have been better."

I was out of the chair and on my knees before Kate before I could even question what I was about to do. Cautiously, I took Kate's hands in mine. She was still weird about letting me touch her, making my desire to bring us both pleasure even more acute in the past weeks and months.

"Is there any baby in the world who has been wanted for as long as this baby has?" Pulling one of my hands from Kate's hands, I reached out and placed my palm flat against the bump. I could feel our son moving within. Despite my need to make Kate feel better, I couldn't help but smile at the feel of him, restless and ready to get on with his life. "We dreamt of this baby ten years ago. And he might not have been conceived in quite the situation either of us had envisioned, but we always knew we wanted him. And when he gets here, when he gets older, we're going to tell him just how long we waited on him."

I could see Kate's eyes grow glassy. She sniffed, determined not to let tears fall.

"I feel like your mother will come around. I can't imagine that she could take one look at her grandson and not want to love him like crazy. For certain, between the two of us, he's going to be the most handsome baby that Rainbow Valley has yet to see."

A glimmer of a smile stretched across Kate's lips, and my chest puffed up in response. My hand still on Kate's abdomen, I looked from her face to her stomach. She hadn't moved from my touch, which I took as a major victory. Still, I knew I couldn't push it. I pulled away as I felt our baby give one last kick.

"What are your plans for this afternoon?" I asked.

"I'd planned on going back to the store. There's some new inventory that I need to figure out how to display and…"

She stopped as she took in the sight of my face. No doubt my expression was skeptical. Standing, I held out my hand. She allowed me to pull her to her full height. As I looked down at her, the urge to pull her close to me and press my lips to hers was overwhelming.

"I think instead that you should go home and get some rest. Call it a day. The inventory will be there tomorrow and you've had a day."

At first, she opened her mouth, and I awaited the argument, but instead, she nodded.

"Everly can cover for me today."

"That's my girl." I bit my tongue after I'd said the words, but she only smiled sadly and turned, walking out of the office.

I was determined to do whatever was possible to make that woman the happiest woman on the planet.

WHEN I PULLED into the parking lot of Old Things New, there were only a couple of cars parked before the storefront. Hopefully, this would mean that Everly wouldn't be busy and she could help me with the side project I'd been contemplating since Kate had left my office.

Inside the store, the few customers inside seemed to be browsing and weren't in any need of assistance. Everly stood behind the counter as she usually did, staring at a laptop but ever aware of every person who stepped into the shop.

"She's not here," Everly said as I approached the counter. Looking up at me from the screen, she squinted. "But you knew that already, didn't you?"

Kate had told me that Everly had an almost superhuman ability to read people.

"I actually came to see you," I said, leaning on the counter and looking over the shop before me. Kate had done an excellent job with the place. As Kate had told me, there were three routes you could go with an antique shop. One was just to let it be a complete free-for-all. Junk everywhere. This appealed to the pickers and treasure hunters who wanted to sift through the madness and find the treasure they were looking for.

Then there were the "we're just pretending to be an antique store" type shops that had a few antiques spread around the store, but mostly sold new items that leaned into whatever the current decorating trend was. Whether that was farmhouse decor or scented candles, you'd find more new items than old. Sometimes you'd find old items that had been repurposed, but the store would only be an antique shop in the vaguest definition of the term.

Then there was the other type of shop, which was the category that Old Things New fell into. A curated antique shop. A shop where someone might find a treasure they were looking for, as well as be able to furnish their house with the curated selection of antique furniture and doodads that graced the sales floor. Not only that, but there were just enough items that didn't fall into furniture or housewares that you could also leave with a gift that was wholly unique. Depending on where you stood inside the shop, you might feel you had slipped into either Regency England or turn of the century America. There was something for everyone in Old Things New.

But there was one thing that I knew wasn't there, but Old Things New was also the only place I had a chance of finding it.

"You remember those books that she sold a few months back?" I asked.

Everly grinned devilishly. There was something about the grin that reminded me of when my brother and I used to devise some half-witted scheme and attempt to get away with it. Seeing it made me realize I hadn't called Adam in over a week. Perhaps I would run by the orchard and pick up some cider for Kate on the way home.

"I like how you ask that question as if I could ever forget," she said, closing the laptop and giving me her full attention. "Those books were the true casualty of your fallout. Do you know how long she held onto those books? Years, Matthew. Years."

"If you're trying to make me feel horrible about it, please let me save you the trouble. I've never stopped feeling horrible about it." In the weeks after I'd found out about the books, I'd envisioned the scenario over and over in my mind. How she'd held onto them and held onto some hope that the baby she had dreamed of would eventually materialize. When she'd sold them, she'd not known she was pregnant yet. In her mind, that dream of a child had died the minute I'd broken her heart.

When I thought about it, my heart pounded at the thought that she'd only ever considered making a baby with me. But then, just as quickly, my heart would stutter at the thought that she'd given up the hope of ever meeting that baby. It amazed me that, until today, I hadn't considered the idea that I could get those books back for her.

That I *had* to get those books back for her. On some level, I felt like I was grasping at things - the house, the books - to repair a wrong that had occurred years ago and had been made worse by my attempt to try to recapture the past.

"You're an idiot, but you love her, don't you?" Everly asked, pulling me from my reverie.

"I doubt that there's any sentence that better encapsulates the last ten years of my life," I said. I was an idiot in love. On most days, I could broker deals that left other agents fuming and jealous as hell. I'd been able to take my business from nothing to the top agency in Rainbow Valley in less than six years.

There were many places where I proved I had more than my fair share of intelligence. But mention Kate's name and I became a fool. Ted Palmer had counted on that fact and it had nearly worked. I suspected that he still had a rabbit up his sleeve, but what he hadn't counted on was Kate. What none of us had counted on was Kate. She had bested all of us.

"Be patient with her," Everly said, doing that thing where she read the other person before her. "I know she tries to be all ballsy and independent, but she needs you. Don't give up on her."

"I have no intention of giving up on her and I can be patient for years. She's earned that from me." Even if it killed me, which was seeming more and more like a real possibility every day.

"She has earned it," Everly agreed, turning back to the computer and flipping the lid. "And if you get out of line again, this time, I will destroy your whole life with nothing more than a few clicks of a mouse. Now, let me find the name and address of the couple who bought those books."

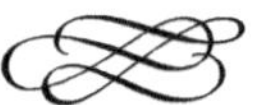

CHAPTER 21

KATE

As much as I hated to admit it, going to Matthew with my problems had been the right choice. He'd listened. He'd soothed.

He'd been the man I had fallen in love with.

What I couldn't understand was how that man had thought it wise to deceive me in order to help Ted Palmer.

I'd taken Matthew's advice and made my way home after I left his office. After the argument with my sister and mother, I was still wound up. Wanting to do nothing more than to wash the worries away, I'd run a bath and sunk into the bubbles with the intention of letting the world turn without me none the wiser. The warm water worked its way across my body, soothing what Matthew's words hadn't already. I sunk further down into the water, determined to lap up every bit of heat from the water possible. As my hands ran over the bump, the memory of Matthew's hand there pushed my thoughts in another direction.

There was, unfortunately, one tension that a warm bath wouldn't solve. If anything, it seemed only to further exacerbate it. My hormones had taken a turn for the crazed, making me feel like I was only fifteen years old again. Being near Matthew and having him put his hands on me was doing nothing to help matters, either.

My hands slid over my abdomen and rested on my clit. Settling back against the tub, I closed my eyes and began to caress, pinch, and work the swollen flesh. As my breath grew more labored, I thought of Matthew's hand on me earlier. If he had moved down just slightly, would I have had the fortitude to stop him? Would I have let him bring me release?

My thoughts became tangled with his phantom voice, coaxing me on. I could almost hear him urging me forward. 'That's it, Kate. Almost there.'

The thought of his voice in my ear brought me to my release, my legs shaking in the water as my pussy clenched. As my breathing returned to normal, I opened my eyes and looked, almost expecting Matthew to be standing there, watching me. The thought sent me on another rollercoaster of need and frustration.

What would it hurt? I thought as I rose from the tepid bath. After all, he said he was here for me. This was a need, just like vitamins or a nutritious meal. Surely stress wasn't good for the baby and the damnable way I needed him was definitely making me stressed. Toweling off, I made my way to the living room and checked the time.

Matthew would be home in less than an hour.

I checked myself in that thought. He wouldn't be home. He would be in my house. I couldn't start thinking of this as a situation where we were playing house. He was simply staying near in case something happened. It had been a lapse in judgment to let him come stay with me, but now that we were there, it seemed pointless to turn the ship around. If I threw him out, he was damn well likely to try to sleep on my doorstep. The man was stubborn. And I knew, despite it all, that he wanted to see me safely through this pregnancy. Not only for myself but also for our child.

For that, I couldn't blame him.

But one thing I didn't have to do was invite him to my bed. I didn't have to let him touch me. I didn't have to let him push himself inside me, over and over and over…

Dammit.

By the time I heard his car pull up in the driveway, I'd decided that I wouldn't give in to the raging need that seemed to take over my body. I was going to have to find a different way to relieve my stress. For a minute, I'd been tempted to find something more alluring to wear, tempting him to push me toward the choice I didn't want to make for myself.

Eventually, I'd come to my senses and threw on a pair of unassuming plaid pajama pants and a tank top. The tank top barely covered my middle, almost giving me the appearance of a man with a gut in a wife-beater. At least that's what I told myself. I doubted Matthew would see the resemblance.

As the key turned in the lock, I cursed the day I'd given him a key. It seemed the sensible thing to do. God forbid something happened and he need to get into the house and I'd been too stubborn to even give him a key. Now? I was half tempted to move furniture before the door and bar him from entering the house, certain that my resolve would falter the minute I laid eyes on him.

I hadn't been wrong.

He'd shed his jacket on the drive over, leaving him in his white button-down with the sleeves rolled up. The effect showed off the toned, thick forearms covered with a light dusting of dark hair. His long, slender fingers only conjured thoughts of the piss-poor job I'd done of bringing myself to completion. He could do more skilled work with his impressive digits. They were the fingers of a piano player, though as far as I knew, he'd never touched the instrument.

But I knew from experience that they were more than capable of playing me.

As he stepped in and placed his jacket on the armchair near the door, he looked over at me, his eyes roaming over me as if taking an inventory. It was something he did more often than I think he realized. Constantly assessing and checking on the woman who was carrying his child. As much as I wanted to say the action annoyed me, even in my less amorous mood, it made me feel watched after and protected. I hated that the feeling made me feel so warm.

But now, his roving eyes just reminded me of what I'd wanted him to do to me before I'd come to my senses.

And I had come to my senses. Hadn't I?

"Feeling better?" he asked. Each day that he came home, I could feel that tension, that desire that he kept in check, to come to me and touch me. Even if only briefly. When we'd been younger, we'd barely been able to keep our hands off one another. If we were at his family's house, we couldn't resist passing through a room without a fleeting touch of a shoulder or a forearm. In the car, his hand was on my leg and mine was running across his arm. If we ran to the store together, we did so hand-in-hand. And when we fell into bed together, we were so close that there was barely a space for a breath between us.

When we'd come back together the night I'd conceived, that same need to touch and be touched took over once again. I could still feel his hand in mine and the way he reluctantly pulled away from me as he left for his car before I would find out the truth of what had brought him to my doorstep.

The thought of that should have dampened my need for him, but it seemed more like the buzzing of a housefly in a faraway room. I knew it was there, but it was too far away for me to do anything about it.

"I need you to help me with something." Damn. The words were out of my mouth before I'd had the chance to reel them back. My hormones were taking over my brain, and I was out of the driver's seat. Fantastic.

"Anything, Kate," he said, coming over to the sofa and sitting down on the other side. He was doing his best to keep his distance, but it was still too close. I could feel the heat of him next to me. I could smell that clean, masculine scent that was all Matthew King. It took all my willpower not to close my eyes and take in a heavy, deep breath, drowning in the scent of him.

"I..." I started, but I wasn't sure how I could put into words what it was I needed from him. This was bound to be a disaster, but it seemed it wasn't one that I could avoid. "I don't know how to ask for it."

"What's wrong, Kate?" he asked, his voice now deeper and somewhat grave, as if he expected me to say something awful. He edged closer to me on the sofa. It should have made me feel horrible that I had caused him any worry. There was no telling what was going through his mind at this point. But the only thing I could concentrate on was how deep his voice had grown and how close he was to me now.

"There's nothing wrong. I just need something, but I don't know that it's fair to ask it of you."

"Kate, you know that if there's anything I can do to make this easier for you, I'll do it in a heartbeat."

"It's just that…" This was insane. I couldn't even get the words out.

"Kate…"

"My hormones are out of control, okay? I can't even think straight!"

I watched as Matthew's face went slack. He said nothing, staring at me as if I'd grown another head.

Idiot. I was an absolute idiot.

"Forget it," I said, standing and making my way toward my bedroom. "It was stupid to say anything. I'm just going to go to bed and…"

I stopped as I felt Matthew's hand clasp around my own. Just the touch alone made electricity shoot up my arm. Still, I was embarrassed, and I knew from the heat I felt in my face that I was blushing like a schoolgirl. I didn't want to look up at him, but when he reached out and pulled my face to look up at his, I no longer had a choice.

"You just surprised me, Kate." His voice was low but tender. My heart stuttered at the sound of it. If I wasn't careful, I could fall right back into that trap where I believed that we'd be something that wouldn't come to a screeching halt. Again. "You know I'm here for you."

My eyes searched his face. I could see the naked hope there and knew that it was damned dangerous to keep going forward.

But I was already carrying his child. Perhaps the best solution was to just do it. Get it over with and move past it already. After all, my hormones weren't going to play nice. If I didn't do something soon, I might wind up in his office later in the week, humping him while he attempted to sell a client a three bedroom-two bath.

"It can't be anything other than mechanical," I whispered, hoping that I sounded forceful enough. "Just one person helping another. One of which happens to be pregnant."

"With my baby," he finished. Something about the way he said it, so possessive, his voice low and seductive, made that ache down below grow even more painful.

With my hand in his, he pulled me toward my bedroom. "Come with me, Kate. I'm going to take care of you."

CHAPTER 22

MATTHEW

When I'd arrived back at Kate's place, I wasn't sure what to expect. I'd been high on the fact that Kate had come to me for comfort after her argument with her sister and mother. That high had quickly been dampened by the fact that the aunt and grandmother of my unborn child thought of him as a mistake. The thought was enraging. I'd had half a mind to find both of them and put the fear of God into them before I convinced myself that doing such would only make things worse for Kate.

Instead, I'd thrown myself into contacting the owners of the books. So far, I had gotten no bites from either my calls or my emails, but given what I was prepared to offer them, I was certain they'd see merit in eventually returning my calls.

By the time I'd pulled up to the curb before Kate's house, I'd gotten my emotions under control. I still wanted to throttle both the women who had hurt Kate, but I'd swallowed the fury, determine not to let Kate know just how angry I was with her family.

When I'd stepped into the house, Kate was nervous and fidgety, seeming unable to get comfortable on the sofa. Over the last few weeks, she'd been growing a little more restless, but I'd chalked it up to her body changing with the pregnancy.

Now, she had moved to the edge of the sofa just as I'd stepped inside the door, watching me warily. At first, I considered that she was still feeling off about what had happened with her mother and sister. After all, it wasn't often that your sister and mother insinuate that the child growing inside you was a mistake.

So when she'd basically told me, her face growing red, but her eyes blazing, that she needed me to make love to her, my brain had over-heated and shut down like an old desktop computer.

In my mind, I knew she wasn't exactly asking me to make love to her, but that was precisely what I planned to do.

Leading her to the bed, I stopped just short of it and pulled at the ill-fitting tank top she was wearing. As my fingers grazed the taut skin of her abdomen, I could see her worrying her lip, wondering if she had made a mistake in asking me to assist her. I knew she couldn't be completely emotionally unaffected by what we were about to do, but I knew she was going to try her best. Any wayward move on my part and she just might send me packing, no matter how badly she needed me. I pulled the top over her head, revealing her breasts to me. Her nipples were taut and pebbled, begging to be suckled. Leaning forward, I took one angry peak in my mouth, licking and caressing her as her hands rose to my shoulders. A moan escaped her as my hand went to her other breast, my mouth never leaving her.

"Matthew, I need…" Her words were harsh, barely more than a whisper.

"I know."

Laying her down on the bed behind her, my hands grazed over the swell of her stomach, my lips following over the slope until my kisses landed just above that wet, damp center that needed my attention so badly. I hooked my fingers into her waistband, pulling the crude pajama pants as well as her panties from her and tossing them behind me. Naked and writhing, that was how I wanted her.

Her pussy was swollen and wet, desperate for attention.

"Poor baby," I said, my voice rough. My hands skimmed the outside of her thighs. She was nearly bucking toward me, desperate for my touch. "Let me take care of you, sweetheart."

My lips met with the wet flesh between her legs and it only took seconds for her to come, her legs shaking and her slick heat clenching, desperate to be filled.

As she came down from her first release, I tore off my own clothes and settled down beside her, turning her onto her side. My right hand roamed over the slopes of her body as my left bicep provided a pillow for her head. Carefully positioning her leg over my own, I slowly pushed into her hot, wet heat. Kate released a near guttural growl as I filled her, her walls grasping at my length as I slowly pulled back and pushed into her once again.

We found our rhythm almost instantly. It was a new experience, pushing into a pregnant Kate, filled with the life we had created not all that long ago. My hands roamed over her breasts, her stomach and back down to her clit as her own body pushed back against my desperate rhythm.

"You're made for me, Kate," I told her, no longer able to control my mouth as I pushed in and pulled out of her. "You feel so damn good. Come for me again, baby. Let me feel you come."

The words were magic. Seconds later, her pussy quaked and shook, pulling my own release from me only seconds later. Spilling inside her, I allowed that primal satisfaction to take hold as I claimed her already taken womb for my own once again. As our breathing returned to normal, I held Kate to me, still inside her, unwilling to let her go.

Moments later, I could feel her body shaking. Rising up, I looked over at her face only to see her cheeks tear-stained.

"Oh, God, Kate." I slid free from her even though I didn't want to. Turning her onto her back, I did an inventory of her body, caressing and touching and trying to see where it was I had caused the hurt. I thought I had been so careful. "How did I hurt you? What's wrong?"

A heavy weight seemed to settle in my stomach as I looked down at Kate's face, her cheeks wet and her eyes closed. She brought her hands to her face, intent on hiding her tears from me.

"You didn't hurt me, Matthew." Her voice was barely above a whisper.

"Then tell me what's wrong, Kate." My hands were still moving over her, the touch no longer sensual as I tried to soothe her.

"I want this so bad." Her words made a flare of hope ignite in my chest. That flare was quickly trampled by the sight of her so distraught, however.

"You can have this, Kate. I swear to you. I'm yours."

"I'm so afraid. Afraid that another day will come and you'll throw me away. Or that you'll not be honest with me like you were the night I got pregnant."

My gut clenched. My heart broke again. Gathering Kate into my arms, I held onto her, but a gaping void presented itself before me. How could I ever make the woman in my arms trust me again?

CHAPTER 23

KATE

$\mathcal{I}$t was inevitable, seeing as I was about to deliver a King grandchild, that they would invite me back to family dinners at the King's house. Though I'd seen Sophie occasionally out and about and had run into Adam not all that long ago, I'd somehow missed Matthew's mother.

The last time I'd seen her was when we'd made our devil's bargain. Now the truth was out. I'd kept my end of the bargain. She had not.

I wasn't angry with her. In hindsight, I wasn't sure that my request of her was the right decision. I'd not only wanted to save Matthew's relationship with his mother, I'd also wanted to prove that ours was true.

What I'd wound up proving was that Matthew wasn't able to set aside his pride and come to me. And it was that reason - among others - that I had been keeping him at arm's length.

"There's no reason to be nervous," Matthew assured me as we made our way up the steps to the King home. The nostalgia of approaching the front door with Matthew made me feel as if I was having an out-of-body experience. The house itself had changed little. There'd been some landscaping done and a fresh coat of paint on the wood siding, but otherwise, it looked the same as it had the first time

Matthew had brought me to a family dinner. Then, I'd been nervous as well, but for an entirely different reason. That time, I'd envisioned both of us stepping toward a hopeful future. Now, I simply saw us stepping toward some sort of doom.

"They've never stopped loving you."

At that, I looked up at Matthew. I wanted to ask him if he ever had. I'd never stopped loving him. Even when I'd been at my most disappointed or heartbroken, I'd never stopped loving him. Had he stopped loving me?

He must have sensed the turmoil in my expression, because he began to say something. Only he was cut short by the door being thrown open by Matthew's mother.

She'd aged gracefully, just as my mother had. However, there was a softness she had that my mother did not. Something that spoke of a willingness to let life happen instead of fighting it. She'd had her fair share of heartache. Even though I'd never met Matthew's father, his absence still hovered around her.

I didn't have time to contemplate what sort of welcome was awaiting me as she pulled me into her arms.

"It feels like my own daughter has finally come home," she whispered in my ear as she clung to me. Her eyes went to my expanding middle. I wasn't huge yet, but I was obvious. "And my second grandchild."

I swallowed a lump that formed in my throat, afraid to look around and see Adam standing near. The reminder that the first King grandchild had been lost so tragically made my heart clench. When I felt Matthew's hand on my lower back, I didn't pull away. It seemed to be the only thing anchoring me to the spot.

Finally, Matthew made some off-the-cuff remarks and pushed past his mother and into the house, with his mother following us. As soon as we walked into the dining room and Mrs. King busied herself in the kitchen, he leaned down to whisper in my ear.

"Sorry about that. Try not to let it worry you. She's never got over losing that grandbaby."

"I can't imagine she would."

It was intimate, him whispering in my ear. His hand on the small of my back. It felt right, which made it all the more terrifying.

"Freaking finally, you dork!" Sophie bounded into the dining room, making a bee-line to me. "Do you know how damn much I've missed you?"

She dragged me into a hug.

"Dinners have been unbearable without you," Sophie said, causing me to snort out a laugh.

"Really, Sophie?" The tall, muscular man who made his way behind her towered over Sophie and me. "I didn't know we were such a chore for you."

He softened as he looked at my face. "Though you have been missed."

Quickly, his eyes slid to my midsection and then swiftly away, as if he had seen something he hadn't meant to see. If Matthew or Sophie noticed the quick movement of his gaze away from my abdomen, they said nothing. Instead, they led me into the dining room where we were presented with a home-cooked meal that put anything I'd eaten recently to shame. At least once I was sitting down, Adam didn't have to strain to look away from that part of me that caused him so much pain to see.

"I'm sorry about your friend," Adam said once we had tucked into our meals.

"Oh God," Sophie moaned around a bite of meatloaf. "Did something happen to Everly?"

I laughed and also marveled that Sophie knew so much about my life. Everly hadn't been a feature in my life when I'd last been attending King family dinners. Still, as plugged into social media as Sophie was with her cosplay page, I wasn't surprised that she knew Everly. Likely, Matthew had also given her a rundown of my life post-Matthew King.

"She's fine." Adam squirmed in his seat and, despite the earlier weirdness, I felt like he somewhat deserved the hot seat treatment.

"He and Everly kinda got into it the other day," I added when Adam didn't elaborate.

From the head of the table, I saw Matthew's mother perk up. Apparently, I hadn't been the only one who thought the exchange was interesting.

"What happened?" Sophie asked, leaning forward in her seat.

"Everly is a social media maven," I explained.

"Oh, I know." Sophie preened at having the inside information on at least this facet of the story. "The engagement on your Instagram is downright staggering for an antiques page, no offense."

"None taken," I said with a laugh. She wasn't the only one who was amazed that a bunch of pictures of antiques had so much interest online. "It's all Everly. She's a wizard with the whole social media thing. So when I ran into Adam with Everly in tow, I suggested she create a social media presence for him."

Matthew sucked in a breath beside me, but I wasn't sure why.

"That's a great idea, Adam! You should do that." Sophie was animated, nearly popping, at the idea of Adam having success online.

"You damn well know I have no intention of doing that, Sophie." The fierceness of Adam's words caught me off guard but didn't seem to annoy Sophie at all, who simply shrugged. "Facebook, Twitter, Instagram. All of it can kiss my ass."

"Adam." The admonition from his mother seemed to at least make him quiet down some, but as I looked between the players at the table, I wondered why the vehemence. Seeing my confusion, Adam sighed.

"When Jessica and I lost our baby," he began and my gut twisted. I stealthily brought my hand to my stomach. Next to me, I could feel Matthew follow the movement with his eyes and hoped he wouldn't bring Adam's attention to it. "When I lost Jessica, people online were merciless. At first, it wasn't bad. So many people - people I didn't even remember - had nothing but well wishes. I didn't pay too much atten-tion to it at all. I was too…"

For a minute, he drifted off, and I forgot to breathe as I watched grief and sadness play over his features.

Recalling that he had been in the middle of a sentence, he started again. "Anyway, at some point, the well wishes turned to speculation. Then there was just cruelty. They said she hadn't been taking care of herself. They said that she was unfaithful. They said all sorts of cruel and untrue things. Simply because they could."

My heart stuttered in my chest. No wonder he wanted nothing to do with anything online. His greatest heartbreak had become fodder for people to express the cruelest facets of their nature.

"I'm sorry, Adam. I didn't know."

"No, I wouldn't imagine you would." Adam's voice sounded resigned. Then he shook his head, as if shaking away a host of memories and ghosts that clung to him. "And I wouldn't imagine that Everly would either. I should find a way to make it up to her."

Sophie pursed her lips and I could see the glint of something in her eye. She shared a glance with me and then looked back at her plate. It was a look I recognized. The one of a woman who saw an opportunity, but knew she'd have to wait to pursue it until later.

When the plates were cleared and Matthew and Adam had disappeared into another area of the house, the moment of truth came. Matthew's mother cornered me. I took a deep breath, wondering what was to come.

"I'm glad you're back. I always felt like you belonged in our family."

"I don't..."

"I know." She held up a hand, and I seemed powerless to continue at the sight of it. "Things between Matthew and you are strange. But I have faith. You two always seemed meant to be."

I said nothing, knowing that it was pointless to argue with her. She wanted what was best for Matthew. No doubt, she also wanted to know that she'd have unlimited access to the child growing inside of me.

"I know you're not saying what you want to. Trust me. I know all the things that you want to say, but Kate. I know you and Matthew. Matthew can be an idiot. But he was always an idiot over you and he always will be. You and Matthew and this baby? You're meant to be."

CHAPTER 24

As the weeks passed, we filled the nights with Matthew inside me, pleasuring me, seeking pleasure himself. It was only fair.

What the nights didn't feature was falling asleep in his arms. I had insisted that we separate once the festivities were over. Sex was one thing. Allowing him to hold me after the deed - despite what had happened during the moment of vulnerability after the first time - was a level of intimacy I wasn't willing to risk.

I knew that Matthew wanted me physically. Hell, I didn't doubt that Matthew wouldn't jump at the chance to close that gap and step into the role of not only doting father-to-be but also doting boyfriend. Fiancé. Husband.

Sometimes I could sense him getting frustrated. On the one hand, I couldn't blame him. If the tables were turned, I'm not sure I could have withstood it.

But if the tables were turned, I never would have gone behind his back with Ted Palmer. Even if he grew frustrated with my demands, I was only doing what I had to protect my heart. Too well, I remembered those weeks that had followed his refusal to believe I hadn't sabotaged his chance at design school. And I also remembered how destroyed I was when I found out about his deception with Ted Palmer. Months had passed, but I still had nightmares about it.

At 30 weeks in, I was only a little over a couple of months from the baby being born. After that, I felt certain that there would be less worry over me and more worry over our child. As it should be. Then, I could get back to trying to repair my heart. And with both the birth looming and my sister's wedding, I had little time to spend wondering what would happen if I gave in and risked my heart all over again.

Despite the looming wedding, Everly had pulled together a baby shower at Old Things New one evening after an early close. I knew that Everly tried to involve both my mother and sister. Cassie wanted no part of the planning, citing the fact that she was too busy preparing for her wedding. My mother had at least attempted to act interested in Everly's plan for a baby shower. In the end, however, she'd claimed she was too involved with other stuff to take part and assured her she thought Everly would do a marvelous job.

Everly hadn't wanted to tell me any of this, but she didn't have to. I could have predicted their responses before Everly ever contacted them.

Not that Everly needed their help. She'd gone all out. Caterer. Guests. Gifts. She'd promised there would be no embarrassing games. The announcement that there would just be gifts, food, and hanging out seemed to make everyone feel more at ease. Even my mother seemed to enjoy herself as she mingled with the guests who ranged from well-known customers to Matthew's sister and mother. Everly had debated making it a co-ed baby shower. Ultimately, she'd decided I'd enjoy being away from Matthew's assessing gaze.

"You know I'm always going to ask before I do it," Sophie said as she sat down next to me. At family dinners, she'd been stealthy about feeling the bump and saying hello to her nephew. She knew I was still weird about Matthew's hovering.

Turning, I presented my belly to her. She pressed her hands on either side of the bump, her face lighting up as she felt the life inside moving around. Over the past weeks, the baby had grown even more restless. A part of me wondered how I would deal with him once he became a toddler.

"He's just like Matthew," she said, still looking at my belly. Then, realizing she might have said something that might cause some weirdness, her head snapped up. She looked at me, mouth open, to likely apologize for nothing at all.

"I've already thought the same," I said, preempting any attempt of a needless apology. "How am I going to keep up with him?"

"Well, I know you and Matthew are in a weird sort of stalemate, but no doubt, he'll be there for all of it. Plus, we all know that Aunt Sophie is going to take her nephew off your hands."

"You were such an excellent baby," my mother stated. I hadn't realized she'd been nearby, and neither had Sophie, as she jumped slightly at my mother's raised voice. She'd had more than a couple of mimosas and was now limber-tongued and ready to converse. "Never fussed. Only cried when you were hungry or tired. If you're lucky, he will be as good as you were."

As compliments went, being told I was an exemplary baby wasn't one of those things I had needed to hear. Still, given how few compliments my mother extended in my direction, I took it.

"The baby will be huge," Cassie interjected. "You can tell because of how big Kate is already. No offense, Kate, but you're like a river barge right now."

And as insults went, it wasn't even the worst Cassie had lobbed at me that month, so I let it slide.

Everly, noting the tension that was wafting off Cassie took the reins of the shower and steered me toward opening some gifts. For someone who was routinely accused of trying to be the center of attention by my sister, I felt odd at being the focus of the gifting. At some point, however, the gift opening high took over. Seeing the gifts made me feel a surreal sort of pleasure, knowing that in a few short months, I would meet the baby who would enjoy those gifts.

"Have you settled on a name yet?" Tara Fleming asked. Tara owned the candle shop that book-ended one side of the shopping mall that held Old Things New. Tara was a severe-looking woman with a few kids of her own. I'd noticed she'd enjoyed giving me various tidbits of wisdom throughout the shower, but nothing that was truly irritating. I wondered if she would have some thoughts on whatever name I threw out to the wolves.

As soon as I opened my mouth to inform Tara that I hadn't come up with anything - Matthew and I hadn't talked names yet - Cassie piped up instead.

"Well, she certainly won't name it after his father," Cassie quipped. "They can't stand each other."

She was holding a mimosa-filled champagne glass in her hand, and I felt the urge to knock it out of her hand. Out of the corner of my eye, I saw Matthew's mother nearly speak up, but I spoke up before she could, hoping to save her the trouble.

"That's not even remotely true, Cassie. I don't know why you would say such a thing."

Everly stood, directing everyone to try a slice of the cake that Francesca had provided from her bakery. She gave me a sympathetic look. I returned it, knowing she was doing her best to smooth over the awkwardness that had been growing over the course of the shower.

"It's lemon," Francesca piped up. I smiled back at her, hoping my smile hid the unease I was feeling. My head was throbbing from the need to throttle my little sister and being completely unable to do so. "When Everly contacted me about catering the shower, I knew we had to go with that since she had been so in love with the cake during Cassie's cake tasting."

"Amazing. Somehow Kate even manages to be the memorable one from my own wedding cake tasting."

I knew how it looked to everyone. Cassie came across as a jealous, bitchy harpy. I should have been glad that it was her they focused on and not me, but I was mostly just embarrassed. After all, she was my sister and what did it say about me that my own sister couldn't be happy that I was about to have a baby?

And now that she'd had a few mimosas herself, I had a feeling I was about to be subjected to more of her worst behavior.

"Had it not been for the fact that Kate hadn't fallen into bed with Matthew the minute he showed her some attention again, none of us would be enjoying these fine mimosas. So, bottoms up."

She raised her glass in salute and then turned it up, finishing off the drink.

There were a few murmurs and attempts to take over the conversation. Everly did a good job of steering everyone around the train wreck that was Cassie. I didn't realize that Sophie had my hand until I rose to go to the bathroom.

"Are you okay?" she whispered, her eyes volleying between my stomach and my face.

"Fine." I smiled, hoping it didn't betray just how mortified and upset Cassie's outburst had made me. "Just going to run to the bathroom."

Or two. Or three. I needed to get away and breathe for a second. While I tried not to let my sister's need for constant attention get to me, she'd gotten under my skin twice in recent weeks. I could blame the pregnancy hormones - and certainly, that could be part of it - but I think she had just finally found my weak spot.

Matthew had always been my weak spot and likely always would be.

As I stood, a sharp pain wrenched through my side, causing me to grab the side of my stomach. Sophie was on her feet in a second, her arm around me.

"It's okay. Just a twinge." My voice wasn't very convincing, though. I could hear my breath coming out harshly. Taking a step, the pain increased, and I bent slightly and then backed back into the chair once again.

It took only a few seconds for the room's attention to fall onto me, once again making me feel uncomfortable at being the center of attention. The pain was still there. Not as pronounced since I had sat down, but enough to make me fear something was wrong. Looking up at Sophie next to me, who had fallen into the seat beside me, my expression must have instantly told her everything she needed to know.

"Let's get her to the hospital," she said, looking up at Everly, who I just realized was now hovering over me. "I'll call Matthew on the way to the car."

"I'm coming with you!" The sound of my mother's voice shocked me. She wasn't drunk exactly, but she had a definite buzz. Everly looked at me for confirmation before she nodded to my mother.

"You can ride in the backseat with me, but no one is to say another word to upset her. Is that clear?" Everly said, directing her words to my mother and, I suspected, Cassie.

I couldn't appreciate Everly's tone as another pain sliced through me.

CHAPTER 25

At some point, I was going to have to get another car. Something less sporty. Something that made sense for driving a baby around.

But for the moment, I was grateful for the speed my Porsche could produce. Sophie had insisted on the phone that everything was okay. That Kate was merely not feeling well, but I knew my sister well enough to detect the hint of worry in her voice. She was my little sister, after all. She'd never been in the habit of disguising her worries and fears from her big brother.

As I sped toward Rainbow Valley General, all sorts of possibilities crowded inside my mind. What if the baby was born prematurely? What if something was wrong with Kate? What if she was actually in danger as I made my way to her and my sister was too afraid I'd crash en route to tell me?

The parking lot near the ER was uncrowded. I could see Sophie's car parked near the entrance. The sight of the car both relieved and scared me. Relief that Kate wasn't alone in whatever was going on. Fear because she'd had to be brought here.

As soon as I stepped through the doors, I saw Everly making her way over to me. "She's fine, but let's get you back there to her so you can see for yourself."

I vaguely registered Sophie following behind Everly, both no doubt looking for cracks in my cool. I must have looked crazed to anyone who knew me. Perhaps more so for those who didn't.

Within minutes, Everly had a nurse cornered and, after explaining that I was the father-to-be, they led me back to Kate's room. I could feel Everly right behind me, no doubt itching to see what a state Kate was in.

Kate was sitting up in bed, her mother sitting next to her. Kate looked at me and gave me a shy smile that reminded me of the first time I'd noticed her when she was only 18 and me 19. I felt a physical ache in my arms to walk toward her and pull her to me, but I simply walked toward her and took her hand in mine. Vaguely, I was aware of her mother standing up and walking out as I pulled her hand to my lips.

I knew in the scheme of things, it crossed some invisible line that Kate had sat down. Given the fact that I'd just spent the past thirty minutes in a state of heightened fear, I couldn't bring myself to care. Kate must have sensed the relief wafting off of me because she didn't protest.

"Everything's fine," she said, and, for the first time, I could take inventory of her. They'd hooked her up to various monitors and what appeared to be a saline drip. There was a rhythmic beeping, which I could only assume was Kate's heart rate. It sounded somewhat elevated, but perhaps it was the excitement of the day. Oddly enough, Kate's cheeks were pink. I couldn't resist reaching out and brushing my knuckles against one.

"What happened?" I asked, still unwilling to let go of Kate's hand. Her fingers were curled around my own and just that simple gesture told me she had been scared as well, no matter how well she was covering it now.

"Just a false alarm." Her voice was a little too controlled. Though she wasn't saying so, she'd been terrified. Terrified that something was really wrong. That our son might be born too early or something even worse. Still, I didn't push her. She'd tell me more if I gave her time. And I'd find out more from Everly and Sophie soon.

"Likely just the excitement and stress of the day. I stood up and there was a pain." Those words, so casually spoken, and yet I could hear the terror she'd felt. I knew there was nothing I could do to go back in time and stop it, but I questioned everything just the same. Had I put more stress on her? Was there something I hadn't done to ease some of the strain on her?

When we'd made love - though I wasn't sure that Kate would refer to it as such - I'd played by her rules. I'd seen that she was beyond pleasured and sated. And I hadn't given in to the overwhelming need to pull her to me once it was all said and done and hold her throughout the night. I was certain that if I had, she would have refused any further assistance.

I brought her lunch during the day and ensured she ate properly for both breakfast and dinner. I tidied any clutter in the house before she could question it. I'd also done my best to anticipate when she would be close to her sister and be there if she needed an ear or a shoulder to cry on after the fact.

It wasn't lost on me that she'd been in the company of said sister this evening.

"They're going to keep me for observation for a little longer and then I should be able to go home. Piper is on the way over now. She was with someone else in labor when it all happened and was just able to get away."

I was still holding her hand in both of mine, stroking her knuckles and watching her with a mixture of worry and adoration.

When she dozed off as we waited for Piper, I stepped outside and found Everly waiting for me.

"So I've got her version," I began.

"And let me guess. Her version simply said that it was all a little excitement and would blow over after she went home from the hospital?"

"Something like that."

Everly looked down the hallway toward the waiting area. I had a sneaking suspicion I knew what was coming.

"Everything was going pretty well until Cassie had one mimosa too many. I should have noticed and cut her off."

I couldn't suppress the growl. "Nothing about what happened is your fault. That woman is a terror. Tell me what happened."

And so she did. She told me how Cassie had managed to not only disparage Kate but also tried to insinuate that I didn't care for Kate. By the time Everly had finished the tale, I was ready to rip the woman's head off.

Everly reached out, putting a hand on my arm. "Don't do anything that's going to make life harder on Kate. She still has to attend that wedding and play the dutiful bridesmaid. Think of Kate."

Briefly, I considered pulling every favor I had in town and seeing that, for some inexplicable reason, Cassie's wedding venue was suddenly unavailable. Then I would pay all the guests to find other things to do that weekend. It would be expensive, but it would be worth it.

"The only thing I think of these days is Kate," I told Everly. "I promise you that what I wind up doing won't harm Kate in any way."

That was for certain.

But it was also certain that it would make Cassie fairly unhappy. At least, that's what I was counting on.

When I stepped into the waiting area, I could see her, folded into her seat in the corner, looking down at her phone. Even when she was unaware of anyone watching her, she affected a sullen look. Her bottom lip stuck out in a perpetual pout. It was nearly impossible to find any trace of her that resembled Kate.

She didn't realize I was upon her until I was taking the seat next to her. She rewarded me with an attempt to fold herself further into the chair, inching to get away from me.

"From here on out, you will cease being a bitch to Kate." Over the years, I'd perfected many different tones. The one I used most often in my business was sort of a charming tone. It wasn't false. I liked people and enjoyed making them happy. The charm came easy because I enjoyed seeing people walking away from a deal with a smile on their faces.

The more difficult people - unscrupulous contractors, government officials, and the like — sometimes required a bit more finesse. With them, I sometimes had to act as if I owned the place, whatever that place might be. And that was the tone I was using with Cassie now. She blinked up at me as it took her a few seconds to formulate a response.

"I'm sorry, but since when did you become my father?"

"Thankfully, I'm not." For more reasons than one, I thought. "But I am the father of the child that Kate is carrying. Today won't happen again. I won't allow you to put the woman I love and my unborn child in danger."

"Perhaps if Kate is so fragile, she shouldn't become a mother in the first place," Cassie said. As much as that sentence made me want to throttle the woman before me, I could see the fear in her eyes. She wanted to appear unaffected. She wasn't nearly so badass.

"That right there is the kind of shit you're going to keep to yourself." My voice was low, and I could see that Cassie wasn't immune to it.

"Keep in mind that I know who your fiancé works for, Cassie. You'd hate for me to make your new life difficult."

"Is that a threat?"

"Are you going to continue making Kate's life hell?"

Her silence was answer enough.

"There. That's a girl. Now you can figure out how to behave like a decent human being."

As I stood, she finally spoke.

"I have a question." Her voice was still a little uneven. "If you're the good guy in this scenario, why aren't you married to my sister yet? It would seem for you that should be top priority."

For a moment, I did nothing more than stare down at Kate's sister.

She was fidgeting, but she still met my eye. And for the first time since I'd known her, I saw just a vague resemblance to Kate.

"You know, of all the things you've ever said to me, Cassie, that's the first one that's really made sense."

CHAPTER 26

KATE

After the incident with Cassie, Matthew became even more overprotective. And, as a result, I became even more confused. I tried to convince myself that pushing Matthew away was the best thing to do. I knew I wanted him. Hell, I knew he wanted me. Neither of those things had ever been in question.

The question was how long it could last.

To make matters worse, the pregnancy was playing havoc with my feelings. I'd never considered myself overly emotional, but lately? I was downright sentimental.

Even my mother and Cassie seemed to be on their best behavior after the baby shower. My mother had called me more frequently to check in on me. Once or twice, she'd even stopped in the shop. I racked my memory to remember if she had ever been in the store other than to attend the shower and came up with nothing.

While Cassie wasn't as proactive as Mom, she'd at least grown less aggressive.

Meanwhile, the shop had become my safe place from Matthew's hovering. While part of me enjoyed his concern, there was still that part of me that felt like a clock was ticking down until it all fell apart again. I knew the feeling was due to the growing nervousness I had over the upcoming birth. Soon, I'd be bringing a baby home. I'd be a mother. I'd had months to prepare, and yet everything seemed to be closing in on me suddenly.

As I stepped into Old Things New, I took a deep breath, taking in the scent of old wood and antiques. Some people found it overwhelming. To me, the scent was calming. It made me think of memories and history. Not my own, but of the people who had once owned and loved the things I now sold.

"Smelling the old stuff again?"

I turned, fixing Everly with a mock glare. "Perhaps I'm just enjoying the smell of my freedom."

"The old man hovering again?"

Everly had taken to referring to Matthew as my old man, despite my insistence that he was simply the father of my unborn child. I knew she harbored hope that Matthew and I would eventually work out our differences. That we'd come together not just as co-parents, but also as romantic partners. Before my pregnancy, I'd never realized that Everly had a hidden romantic streak. Matthew realized it before me and had been quick to pounce on it. Much to my chagrin, they'd become partners in crime.

"I appreciate his concern," I said, glossing over the fact that it wasn't his concern that I appreciated most. It was the fear that I would lose my heart all over again. "But I appreciate a moment of stillness."

Making my way toward the office, I made a mental note of the things I needed to accomplish that would make it as easy as possible for Everly to work through my maternity leave.

Of course, the thought of going on maternity leave brought about a fresh round of panic. I pushed the thoughts away, focusing on the shop.

"Well, since that moment of stillness is so appreciated, I suppose you wouldn't mind if I took a moment to run an errand?" Everly asked as she followed me into the office.

Tossing my purse into my desk drawer, I walked back onto the sales floor with Everly close behind. "I assure you that I won't go into labor while you're gone."

I turned to see a shadow of concern flit over Everly's face. I felt like a heel. I knew how concerned Everly had been after the incident at the baby shower. Cassie might have been my sister by blood, but Everly was my sister of the heart.

"Truly, Everly. I'll be fine."

A slow smile spread across Everly's lips. With a promise that she'd be back, she nearly ran out of the shop. Wondering what could cause Everly to sprint out of the shop in excitement, I shrugged, knowing that she would tell me when she was ready for me to know. Maybe all the antics with Matthew and their attempt to push me toward him had led her to find her own romance.

I barely had time to be annoyed with the fact that Everly was possibly keeping potential romantic gossip from me when I noticed the box on the cash counter. The box hadn't been there when I'd walked in and, seeing as we had yet to open, I was certain no one else could have placed it there. Surely we hadn't gained an intruder.

I'd not heard any more about Ted Palmer's antics since the protest. While he obviously had no intention of taking credit for the shenanigans, it surprised me there'd been no other attempts to scare me out of my ownership of the shop. I knew how much he wanted the property and didn't expect that he would give up so easily. Was this his latest salvo?

Gingerly, I stepped around the counter and picked up the box. I wasn't sure what I was expecting. While I knew Ted wanted the property, I also didn't expect he'd be so bold as to resort to a box full of snakes.

Holding my breath, I lifted the lid of the box.

What I found inside robbed me of my breath. I would have been less shocked to find a slithering mass of reptiles.

I reached in, pulling the three books out of the box. The Wonderful Wizard of OZ, The Marvelous Land of OZ, and Tik Tok of OZ. The same books I'd sold to the random customer not long before I'd found out I was pregnant.

Suddenly, all those emotions I'd been trying to keep at bay surfaced all at once. I choked back a sob as I ran my hand over the covers. I'd thought the books were gone forever and here they were, right in front of me. I brushed away a tear before it could fall onto the leather-bound cover of The Wonderful Wizard of OZ.

"I would have saved the books for later if I'd realized they were going to make you cry."

Looking up, I saw Matthew standing near the front door, just as he had the day he'd come back into my life. He must have been in the shop the whole time. No doubt, he and Everly had planned the whole scenario. I should have been upset, but all I could feel was my heart racing in my chest as more tears threatened to fall.

"I sold these." I couldn't think of anything else to say.

"I know. I'd didn't know about the books until Everly told me. When she told me that you'd sold them, I knew at some point I'd have to get them back."

He stepped closer to the counter. He was dressed in one of the tailored suits I knew he always wore to impress clients. His clients weren't the only ones he was impressing. I'd never found him more devastatingly handsome.

"The woman who bought them from you initially didn't want to sell them to me, but when I offered her twice the price, she gave in." He smiled a smile that was so ridiculously charming, I had to bite my lip to force myself not to smile in return. "Of course, there was also the sob story."

"A sob story," I repeated, trying to pull myself together.

"You know. Boy meets girl. Boy is an idiot. Girl hates boy for being an idiot."

"Girl doesn't hate you," I said before he could finish whatever he'd been about to say. Even at my most angry, I'd never hated Matthew. I'd never stopped loving him, much to my continued annoyance.

"Is there a chance I could steal you away?" The way he asked the question reminded me of the first time he'd asked me out on a date. He'd been nervous and I couldn't believe it. There he was. The guy I'd crushed on for years, nervous as he asked me out.

Truthfully, it still amazed me that the boy I'd been so crazy over was crazy over me as well.

"Everly," I began.

"Is around the corner at the cafe. As soon as she sees the car leave, she'll be back over here."

Of course. I'd known as soon as he stepped out of the shadows that they'd planned the whole thing in advance. Why I hadn't seen the admittedly welcome subterfuge was a serious failing on my part.

Matthew held out his hand, waiting for me to accept him. There was something monumental about this moment. Whatever happened in the next few minutes and hours was going to set the tone for the rest of our lives. I didn't know how I knew that, but the feeling was palpable.

Stepping around the corner, I took Matthew's hand. I forgot about my handbag, the books on the counter, and the inventory of the shop around me. I forgot about everything but the feel of Matthew's hand in mine.

He led me to his car. As we rolled through the streets of Rainbow Valley, we said little. Tension blanketed the car like thick smoke.

Matthew King was nervous.

And before long, I realized why he was nervous.

Because I realized where we were headed.

Pulling into the drive of the Richardson Estate, memories flooded my mind. Memories of all the times we had dreamt about the house when we were younger. Memories of skulking around the place like a couple of thieves.

But the most potent memory was that of the night when we'd made the life that was growing inside me.

After he parked, he didn't give me a chance to ask questions. Instead, he jumped out and made his way round to the passenger side. When the door opened, he once again offered his hand.

I had questions. Lots of them. But instead of voicing any of them, I simply accepted his hand.

As he led me toward the steps of the house, I could see that some sort of construction had recently begun. 2x4s lay stacked near one side of the house. Empty paint buckets sat nearby, depleted of their contents.

Once we came to the door, he didn't fumble for a key. My gut twisted as I remembered the deception of that night, but I pushed it aside for the moment. The pain now seemed dull and unimportant. As if realizing where my mind went, Matthew turned to me with a sigh. His expression was one of full contrition.

"The only thing I've ever wanted out of this was you, Kate." Ignoring the open door behind him, he reached out, cupping my jaw. I leaned into his touch, desperate for the feel of him against me. The nights he'd left me pleasured and sated, I'd never let myself truly fall into his touch like this.

He lingered for only a moment. Then, he reached down and took my hand once again. Pulling me into the foyer of the house, I marveled at the metamorphosis.

The house was still devoid of most furniture, though I spied a small sideboard along the wall in the living area. However, it was apparent that the basic cosmetic defects had been patched up.

"I only had them fix the foundational defects," he explained as he watched me take in my surroundings. "Basically, I had them make it livable. I wanted you to make any final cosmetic decisions."

The last time I'd been in the house, it had been too dark to take in most of the minor details. Furthermore, I hadn't been all that interested in my surroundings that night.

As I looked over at Matthew as he watched me, I realized I still wasn't.

I let him lead me around the house, showing me room after room. The plumbing in the kitchen had been updated, he explained. He also updated the bathrooms with more modern fixtures while keeping to the vintage aesthetic. When he finally led me to what would have been our bedroom, I saw that there was one other piece of furniture he had placed in the house.

The bed was a large, four-poster bed. Amazingly, the room was large enough to accommodate the large piece of furniture. It had been dressed with a basic white quilt, but other than that, it was a blank canvas.

"You're the one with the eye for decor," he explained. He was still a little nervous. Not used to seeing Matthew nervous, it made me wonder if the house was the only thing he was nervous about. After all, I'd known for a while he had bought the house with this intent.

"If you don't like the bed, we can change it." Reaching out, he took my hand. Then, he stood before me. Taking my other hand, he looked down at our entwined hands and then back to me. "I don't know how to prove to you it's always been you I've wanted, Kate. I've been a massive idiot."

In the past, I would have likely agreed with him simply to rile him. Right now, however, it felt like everything depended on what he would say next.

"I never gave up on the dream that we had together. I want to come home to you every day. Not like the way I do now. I want to come home and pull you into my arms. You can tell me about your day and I'll tell you about mine. I want to go to bed with you every night and wake up next to you in the morning. I want Christmas morning with our kids and summer picnics in the backyard.

"But more than anything, I just want you, Kate."

As he reached into the inner pocket of his jacket, I realized I was holding my breath. When he pulled out the small box, I let my breath out in a whoosh. He fumbled with the box for a moment before he opened it and revealed the ring inside. The ring was easily over a hundred years old. I recognized the setting and style as one that was more popular around the turn of the century. Antique jewelry wasn't my expertise, but I recognized quality when I saw it.

And I knew Matthew knew I would as well. He'd known I would want an older ring. I didn't have time to contemplate the choice of the ring before he went down on one knee. I'd envisioned this moment more times than I could count.

And none of those dreams had ever seemed as perfect as this moment. In the house we'd dreamt of. In the bedroom we'd planned to wake up in for the rest of our lives. With our first child growing inside me. And the man I loved looking more perfect than he had ever looked.

"Kate Cavanaugh, despite my many shortcomings, you must know that I'm hopelessly in love with you. I have been since that day I first noticed you all those years ago. I promise you I'll spend the rest of my life making you happy. Making you feel loved. Listening to you. Worshiping you. Will you marry me, Kate?"

I pulled in a deep breath. Had I not, there was the real possibility I might have teetered and given into the overwhelming pull of my emotions at that moment.

"Stand up," I breathed.

I couldn't ignore the look of worry and concern as Matthew slowly stood up, still holding the ring in his hand. But I needed the man before me to stand. I needed him to lean on at that moment when all the world seemed to spin out of control as it finally, finally, came to its right conclusion.

"Kate?" Matthew asked, and there was no disguising the worry in his voice.

"I need you to hold me, Matthew. Otherwise, I might just fall over."

The look of worry turned to one of concern as he quickly gathered me in his arms.

"Do you need to go to the ER? Are you in pain?"

I shook my head with a smile. "I'm fine, Matthew. It's simply not every day that the man I've been in love with since 10th grade asks me to marry him."

Matthew sucked in a breath and drew me closer to him. Looking down at me, a plethora of emotions crossed his face.

"Does this mean…?" He couldn't finish the sentence.

"Yes, Matthew. I'll marry you."

He released a puff of air that was part laugh and part sigh of relief. He brought his lips to mine, teasing at a kiss before pulling away and resting his forehead against mine. Looking down, he noticed he still had the ring in his hand. He held my body to him as he maneuvered my hand between us and placed the ring on my finger. I felt drunk with emotion. My body tingled with the joy of what had just occurred, as well as my need for the man standing before me.

"Are they done with the work on the house?" I asked, looking down at the ring on my hand and back up at Matthew.

The question seemed to take him by surprise. "Yes. They completed work on it a couple of weeks ago."

"So no one will come by in the next few hours."

Understanding dawned on his face as he looked down at me. Slowly, a devious grin spread across his face.

"Are you suggesting we test the bed?" he asked, already leading me toward the bed.

"Something like that," I answered as he maneuvered me onto the bed and moved down beside me. "But only if you promise to hold me after and talk about all the things we're going to do with this place after."

I watched as his pupils flared. He understood what I was offering him. In all of our passionate nights together, I'd never let him hold me after. There was little to no conversation in the minutes that followed our release.

Finally, I was allowing the intimacy that I had denied us for so long. While it might have seemed a given with my acceptance of his proposal, the stating of the fact was monumental. He'd needed to hear it and I'd needed to say it.

"I love you, Kate."

"I know," I answered as he pulled me closer to him and claimed my lips with his own.

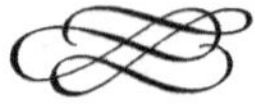

CHAPTER 27

KATE

*B*ig as a house.

My sister hadn't been as annoying in the past month as she had before the incident at the baby shower, but she'd got one last jab in before everything was over.

What she didn't realize was that I was more than pleased with being big as a house. I was pregnant with my first child. And despite the scare a while back, I'd nearly made it all the way through my pregnancy.

I was proud to be as big as a house.

Not that being a massive bridesmaid didn't have its drawbacks. Lauren had done an amazing job with my dress. The peach-colored fabric flowed over the swell of my belly. Matthew had insisted I looked like a goddess.

As I stood before the assembled guests as Cassie said her vows, I found his face in the audience. Our eyes met, and I felt that electric twinge up my spine that felt no less powerful than it had the day I'd first noticed him in high school. His lips quirked up to one side as he noted my gaze on his and I stifled my smile.

Something that wasn't difficult to do as I felt another slight twinge of pain in my lower abdomen. The little squeezes had been irregular and not altogether overwhelming. Still, I turned away from Matthew's stare so that he didn't notice if I possibly grimaced.

Once the wedding was over and everyone was home, I'd let him know. More than likely, it would be a while before we needed to make our way to the birthing center. Having him hover over me during the wedding would make the stress of the day even more pronounced.

When the vows were said and done and everyone made their way to the location of the reception, I breathed a sigh of relief. Only a little while longer. Then I could go home, fold myself into Matthew's embrace, and relax. I was certain that once I did that, everything would calm down. I was still two weeks away from my delivery date and I had every intention of seeing that date come with my still being big as a house.

"I HAVE A CONFESSION TO MAKE."

Looking up at Matthew, I saw that familiar mischievous glint in his eyes. I'd just been marveling at how nearly docile Cassie had seemed in the past weeks. We'd watched as she'd had her first dance with her new husband, beaming up at him. Despite everything, the wedding went off without a hitch. Now, as I stood on the dance floor, dancing with Matthew, all the worries faded into the background.

"I may have put the fear of God into your sister after the baby shower incident."

"Oh, you didn't," I said through a grimace. I'd found my sister's sudden change of heart somewhat odd, but I'd never considered that Matthew might have had something to do with it.

"I'm not letting anyone hurt you again." The mischievous glint was gone and something primal took its place. My breath caught at the sight of his expression. It was the expression of a man who had something he would die to protect. And I knew without him telling me that those two things were currently in his arms.

"Whether it's me or your sister," he continued, and his hold on me tightened slightly. I was certain he wasn't aware of the slight change in his grip on me. "I wasn't just vomiting sweet nothings to you that day. I meant every word."

He was referring to the day that had led to everything that had happened after. When we'd made love in our new house. It hadn't been our house then, but it was now. I'd spent the last few weeks nesting. Deciding on furniture and paint colors. Little had been done yet, but we'd made the bedroom and the nursery a priority. We'd decided on neutral colors for the nursery because neither of us could imagine having just one child at this point. Our dreams had always featured kids running through the yard. Not just kid.

My mind was floating back to that night that we'd conceived when the pain hit. It was more acute, more sudden than the ones before. And I couldn't hide my reaction to it. Gripping Matthew tightly, I leaned my head forward.

"Kate, what's wrong?" His voice sounded hazy and far off as the pain took a deeper hold over my body and I grasped my stomach.

I didn't have to answer. I could feel Matthew sweeping me up into his arms. I was powerless to offer any objections. Looking over his shoulder, I could see my mother following close behind. Hasty instructions and plans were being made between them and others who had followed. I could hear Matthew telling my mother to follow along in her own car.

Once we were inside the car and Matthew was pulling out of the parking lot, I put my head back against the headrest.

"Two weeks early," I managed.

"It will be fine." I could hear the silent statement behind his words. It will be fine because it has to be.

LUCKILY, Matthew was right. It was fine.

Piper was the best midwife in the country. I could say that with ease despite never having known another midwife as far as I was aware. She was there almost immediately and had been a rock to both myself and Matthew.

When the wriggling mass that was our son was pushed out into the world, my focus shifted from the overwhelming emotions I was feeling to Matthew's face. I watched as a storm of expressions crossed his features.

Amazement. Fear. Possession. Love. It had all been there as clear as day as he finally held our son.

The moments after his birth had been busy, and it seemed as if hours passed before I could be alone with my son and his father. As I held the newborn in my arms, Matthew braced behind me. Looking down on the squirming mass, I shifted and turned to look back at him.

"Is it everything you thought it would be?" I asked.

Looking from our son to me, he smiled. "Oh, my love. It's everything I ever dreamt of and much, much more."

EPILOGUE

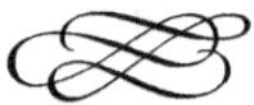

MATTHEW

"**Y**ou know what I've discovered?"

Looking up from the book I was reading, I watched as Kate made her way across the bedroom. I pulled off my glasses and took in the sight of her. It seemed like she had swelled with the new life we had created overnight. After Henry was born, we'd wanted to get started on his sibling as soon as possible, hoping to have them as close in age as possible. It had taken over a year from the time we had begun trying for us to conceive. There had been worry that perhaps Henry was our miracle baby. But then Kate had missed her first period.

And this time, I'd been able to be there for all of it.

"The Wizard of OZ is actually a terrifying story for a three-year-old," Kate said as she positioned herself next to me on the bed.

"I'm not sure it's any less terrifying for a thirty-something," I said, wrapping my arm around her middle and feeling the life inside her move. "I think she moves around even more than Henry did."

"Only slightly," she admitted and then curled against me. "If she's any more active than Henry when she gets to her toddler years, I'm going to have to sell the shop or get a nanny."

Even though she had mentioned such a scenario a few times, I knew Kate wouldn't give up Old Things New without a fight.

"Or I could take a less active role at the agency and become a stay-at-home dad. For the most part."

She turned in my arms, facing me.

"You'd be okay with that?"

"You provide the babies and..."

I couldn't finish my sentence as she pulled me to her and sank her lips to mine. Almost instantly, I rose to the occasion. When she pulled away, I looked down at her.

"Hate to tell you this, Kate," I said, breathing in heavily, "but we can only get one started at a time."

She smiled a lazy smile that still made my heart flip. I could imagine us old and gray and seeing that smile. My old battered heart would still stutter in my chest.

"Remember during my last pregnancy when I asked you to, you know, help me out?"

That stuttering of my heart was met by a slow, warm sensation that flowed over my body. Truth was, I remembered a lot of things about that pregnancy. Some heart-wrenching, some exhilarating, but all amazing.

"I suppose I can help you out, my lady," I said in my best mock British accent. "On one condition."

"What's that?"

"Promise that I get to hold you after until you wake up. Deal?"

"Deal."

ABOUT THE AUTHOR

Chloe Bishop lives in a state of discontent. Luckily, she likes writing romance, so she travels to the land of Romancelandia frequently to get away. She does not appreciate crew cut t-shirts.

www.ingramcontent.com/pod-product-compliance
Lightning Source LLC
Chambersburg PA
CBHW070513160726